CLAIM JUMPER

Bill Turner's ambition was to become a doctor and save lives—not to take them. But when he went to Cripple Creek to help his brother mine for gold, Bill found him dead at the hands of bushwhacking claim jumpers. Determined to punish his brother's killers, he strapped on the dead man's gunbelt and set out to bring justice to the mining community. But the big men in town were dead set against Bill Turner's ideas of fair play, and there was only one way for him to convince them—at the end of a smoking Colt .44!

CLAIM JUMPER

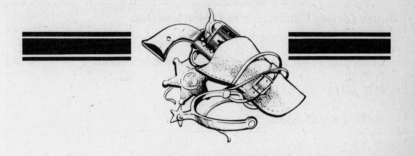

Doyle Trent

ATLANTIC LARGE PRINT
Chivers Press, Bath, England.
John Curley & Associates Inc.,
South Yarmouth, Mass., USA.

Library of Congress Cataloging in Publication Data

Trent, Doyle.
  Claim jumper.

  (Atlantic large print)
  Originally published: New York City: Leisure Books, c1981.
  1. Large type books. I. Title.
  [PS3570.R398C4 1984]   813'.54   83–15282
  ISBN 0–89340–635–X (J. Curley)

British Library Cataloguing in Publication Data

Trent, Doyle
  Claim jumper—Large print ed.—(Atlantic large print)
  I. Title
  813'.54[F]   PS3570.R/

  ISBN 0–85119–613–6

This Large Print edition is published by Chivers Press, England, and John Curley & Associates, Inc, U.S.A. 1984

Published by arrangement with Dorchester Publishing Co, Inc

U.K. Hardback ISBN 0 85119 613 6
U.S.A. Softback ISBN 0 89340 635 X

CLAIM JUMPER

CHAPTER ONE

The constant lurching of the passenger car slowed as the train started up Ute Pass. The air turned suddenly cooler. The small boy across the aisle from Bill Turner had finally stopped crying and was sleeping in his mother's arms. A whiskered, overall-clad gent in the seat ahead turned toward Turner and allowed, 'We're agittin thar.'

Bill Turner shifted his weight on the hard seat and straightened his legs as much as the seat ahead would allow. Two days on a train and it seemed like a week.

The Santa Fe had carried him and the other passengers as far as the new city of Colorado Springs, and they had moved to the smaller Midland train for the rest of the journey to Florissant on the western side of Pikes Peak. The engine was puffing slower and louder than it did on the prairie, and the train was moving at about the speed of a trotting horse. Turner put his head out the window to look up the tracks and immediately got a cinder in his eye.

The woman across the aisle was dozing, still holding the child. Turner felt sorry for

1

her and had twice offered to hold the child for her so she could rest better. She had politely declined.

Turner hoped there would be a doctor wherever the woman and child were going. He wished he could do something for the boy.

The whiskered gent put his head out the window. 'Thar's riders up thar,' he said. Suddenly he jerked his head back inside, his face pale. 'They're wearin' masks. Good gawd, it's a robbery.'

The train came to a halt, brakes squealing. A shot came from behind Turner, and he turned to see a man with a black muffler around the lower half of his face aiming a pistol at him. The bore looked to be as big as the open end of a rain barrel. The shot went harmlessly through the ceiling, but the sound in the closeness of the passenger car made Turner's ears ring.

'No one moves,' the masked man hollered. At the same time, another masked man appeared at the other end of the car, pointing a short, double-barreled shotgun at the passengers. 'Git yore hands up,' he bellowed.

The woman across the aisle was awake.

'What?' she cried. She said no more. Her small son started crying again.

'You,' the shotgun-toting bandit pointed his weapon at Turner. 'Stand up. And keep yore hands in sight.'

Turner stood slowly. His knees were stiff from sitting too long. He said nothing.

'Well, I'll be,' exclaimed the bandit. 'A cardboard collar and a necktie. What kind of man are you? Answer me, dammit.'

'I, uh, I teach,' Turner said, his eyes fixed on the twin bores of the shotgun.

'A schoolmarm. I mean a schoolmarm man.' The shotgun toter's bushy eyebrows went up and he laughed at his own joke. 'Hell, you're big enough to go bear huntin' with a stick, but I'll bet you couldn't whip the mud off yer shirt tail.' He guffawed at that one.

The other gunman spoke next. 'Let's git their money and git. You keep that spray gun on 'em and I'll take their pokes.'

'Let him do it,' the shotgun wielder said. 'He'll do anything we tell 'im to, won't you schoolmarm? That way we'll have two guns on 'em.'

'All right, but let's do it and git.' The bandit was getting nervous. 'Start with yourself,' he said to Turner, 'and git every

3

poke and watch in this car.' He nodded toward the young woman and child. ' 'Cept theirs. We ain't robbin' women and kids.'

The child was crying softly.

Lips clamped shut, Turner reached into his hip pocket and pulled out the cowhide wallet he had carried for years. The pistoleer grabbed it and tossed it into a burlap bag he carried. 'Yer watch too,' he ordered.

'It's not worth much,' Turner protested. 'It's been in the family a long time. It's not real gold.'

'Gimme it.' The bandit grabbed the chain that dangled from Turner's vest pocket and jerked out the watch. Turner grabbed for it. 'You can't have it.'

The pistol barrel came up hard against the side of Turner's head, and he staggered back. The gun was aimed at a spot between his eyes, and the finger on the trigger tensed.

'You got more guts than good sense,' the bandit said. 'One more fool move like that and it'll be your last move on this earth.'

The shotgun toter laughed, a raucous high-pitched whinny. 'Make a believer out of 'im. Feed 'im some lead.'

'Jest do like I told you and start

collectin',' the pistoleer ordered.

Turner said no more. He went from passenger to passenger while the pistol was aimed at the back of his head.

The whiskered gent handed over a small leather pouch tied at the top with a drawstring. 'That's my stake,' he said. 'That's all I got. Without that I got nothin'.'

'Shut up,' the bandit said.

There were only eight men in the car and one woman. Turner collected their wallets, four watches, and two rings and dropped them into the bag.

A shot came from outside the car, and the pistoleer became even more nervous. 'Muley's got his car robbed and he's ready to go. Let's git.'

Another high whinny came from the shotgun bandit. 'Anybody sticks his head outside this car gets it blowed off,' he shouted. He fired a shot into the floor to emphasize his message.

Then they were gone.

*   *   *

A crowd always greeted the Midland Express as it chugged into Florissant, a lumber camp high in the Colorado Rockies. Most of the residents were lumberjacks or sawmill workers who wore lace boots, denim jackets and Scotch caps. Dusk had almost obscured the tracks ahead when someone shouted, 'She's a'comin. I can hear 'er.' A cheer went up as the train puffed and squealed into the station. Handshakers and backslappers gathered around the passengers as they stepped stiffly off the train. A half dozen voices spoke at once, telling about the robbery and why the train was late.

Turner had no more than stepped onto the plank sidewalk when someone yelled, 'He helped 'em.'

The crowd had turned angry at the story of the holdup, and four tough looking lumberjacks surrounded Turner. 'Is that right?' a scarfaced man asked. 'You in on it?' asked another.

'Why, no,' Turner answered, surprised. 'They took my wallet and watch too.'

'They didn't get his money,' a fellow passenger exclaimed. 'He put on a good act and gave 'em his wallet and watch, but he had his money in his shoes.'

'I was advised to keep my money hidden,' Turner said. 'My brother told me to take no chances.'

'Who told you?'

'My brother. Lemual Turner. He was killed at Cripple Creek.'

'Where'd you come from?'

'Garden City. That's in Kansas. I'm going to Cripple Creek to learn what I can about my brother's death. Did any of you know him?'

'Naw.'

The crowd was undecided about Turner, listening to every word that was said, looking him over carefully. Then another voice was heard.

'He ain't no robber. He had to help 'em. They hit 'im over the head and stuck a gun in his face.' It was the whiskered gent in overalls talking. 'They took my poke and left me with nothin' but these.' He held up two silver dollars. 'They didn't look in my pockets, but they took my stake. I was goin' prospectin', and now I got to find a job.'

Hostility faded and the crowd quickly lost interest in the well dressed but weary Bill Turner. 'You don't look like no train robber,' a man said. 'You're big enough,' he said, looking up at Turner's six feet two inches, 'but any man that ain't got no calluses on his hands has to find a legal way

7

to rob folks.'

Another muttered, 'Must be a banker or drummer or somethin'.'

'I'm not a banker nor a salesman,' Turner said. 'I'm a teacher. I'm going to Cripple Creek to try to find out how my brother died. Can any of you tell me when the stage leaves for Cripple Creek?'

'Not till morning,' someone answered. 'They ain't going up that road in the dark.' The crowd walked away, most of them headed for a lantern-lighted saloon a hundred feet away.

It was dark by then and Turner found himself alone on the depot sidewalk. Almost alone. One other figure stood in the dark, looking lost and frightened. It was the young woman, carrying her sick child. Two carpet bags sat at her feet.

In four long strides Turner was at her side. 'Is someone meeting you, ma'am? Can I help you?'

'No thank you,' she said.

Turner noticed that she was pretty, with expressive dark eyes to match her dark hair. But she was obviously worried, and so weary she appeared ready to collapse.

'Ma'am, I just can't leave you standing here. Let me carry your bags. Are you

8

going to the hotel?'

'No, I—' Weariness and worry overcame her then. A single tear ran down her cheek. She sniffed her nose and wiped it away, trying to regain her composure. 'My husband was supposed to meet me here. I wonder if something has happened.'

Turner nodded toward the depot. 'There's a light inside. Must be someone there. Maybe you can wait inside. When your husband shows up, he'll be sure to look for you there.'

He picked up her two bags without waiting for a reply, tucked one under his left arm and picked up his own bag, then led the way to the depot.

A small man with a hunched back was leaving through the depot door when they approached. 'Are you the stationmaster?' Turner asked.

'Yeah.'

'She needs a place to wait for her husband.'

'I was just about to lock up,' said the small man. 'I don't work all day and all night, you know.' He looked at the woman and the child she carried and spoke softer. 'She ought to be at the hotel, not sitting up here.'

'Her husband is supposed to meet her here,' Turner said. 'He ought to be along anytime. He'll look for her here, not at the hotel.'

'Okay,' the small man said. He turned back to the door and opened it. 'I'll light a lantern and stoke up the stove. Gets pretty cool up here at night. I had a daughter about her age. She died of consumption. I wish somebody'd helped her.'

'Don't you have a doctor here?' Turner asked.

'No closer than Cripple Creek,' the stationmaster said.

'Is there a doctor in Cripple Creek?'

'Last I heard there was. My Mable went up there last week to get somethin' for her arthritis.'

The stationmaster studied Turner from his low-cut shoes to the white collar and necktie. 'You look like an educated man. You know anything about doctorin'?'

'No, but if fate is willing, I'm going to learn.'

Leading the way to a hard bench, the stationmaster invited the woman to sit. He took a heavy wool mackinaw off a peg on the wall, folded it and invited her to put the child on it. She did. The child slept.

10

Turner opened the potbellied stove and put a chunk of wood in it. Red coals put a flame to the wood.

'When did you eat last?' he asked the woman.

'This morning. In Colorado Springs,' she said. 'I'm not hungry, but my son needs nourishment. Do you know where I could buy something?'

'At the Grubstake Cafe,' answered the small man. 'That's over by the saloon. Can you walk over there?'

'I'll go,' said Turner. 'What kind of food does the boy like?'

'Something soft,' she said. 'He hasn't been able to hold down much of what he eats. He needs a doctor.' She turned to the stationmaster. 'Is the doctor in Cripple Creek a competent one?'

'I hear he's pretty good. My Mable likes him. What you ought to do, young lady, is get back on this train in the mornin' and go right back to where you came from, or get on the stage and get that boy to the doc in Cripple Creek.'

'Cripple Creek is my destination,' she said. 'But my husband is supposed to meet me here where the railroad ends.' Her voice had a midwest accent.

11

'What's your husband's name?' the small man asked.

'Mike Mahoney. He wrote me and said he had found gold and I should board the next train and come to him.'

'Maybe you're rich and don't know it, young lady. There's gold around Cripple Creek to be found. But you'd better get some grub into that boy.'

'I'll go right now,' Turner said.

Ma Ables' Grubstake Cafe was next door to the saloon so that it could be entered from the saloon or from the street. Turner entered from the street, sat at a wooden counter and glanced around the room filled with wooden tables and chairs. The tables were covered with red-checkered oilcloth.

'You look like you just got off the train,' said Ma Ables, wiping her hands on an apron tied around her ample middle. 'I can give you a good steak. Just butchered yesterday.'

'I have to have something I can carry,' Turner said. 'There's a sick boy over in the depot, and he needs something soft.'

'Something soft. Well, let's see. I got some mashed potatoes still warm, and some home made bread.'

'I don't suppose you have any milk?'

'Yeah, we've got milk. That's why we keep that old Jersey. It's good and fresh, and it's the best thing in the world for a sick child. I know, I raised three of 'em.'

Turner smiled. 'Right now, you're the best friend that child's got. Can I borrow something to carry it in?'

'Got an empty lard can, all clean and purty. And I'll wrap an old blanket around the mashed potatoes to keep 'em warm. Anything else? How about yourself?'

'Oh, yes, there's the child's mother. She needs something.'

'How about a big roast beef sandwich and some coffee? With homemade bread.'

'Nothing could be better.' Turner's smile widened.

Ma Ables went into the kitchen. Cabinet doors slammed and pots rattled as she put together the order. Soon she came back into the dining room carrying two-gallon lard cans, one wrapped in a tattered but clean blanket. She handed them over, along with a flour sack containing two thick sandwiches. 'I made a sandwich for you too,' she said.

'Mrs. Ables, you're wonderful. How much do I owe you?'

'Fifty cents.'

'It's worth twice that much.'

'You just take care of that boy, now.' Ma Ables' face turned pensive and sadness came into her eyes. 'I wish my boys would come back home. I sure do miss 'em.'

CHAPTER TWO

The child was awake and crying again when Turner got back to the depot. But he soon quieted down as his mother spoon fed him the mashed potatoes and milk. She didn't touch her own food until the child had eaten all he was going to eat. 'I hope that's enough for him,' she said. 'I wish I could get him to a doctor tonight.'

Turner ate his own sandwich in silence. He reached inside his coat pocket for the letter, unfolded it and read it for what must have been the twentieth time. He laid it aside, put his head back and let his mind wander.

He recalled the farm, the homestead his father and mother had worked so hard for. Worked so hard their health was ruined. The farm sold for barely enough so that Ma and Pa Turner could only buy a small cabin in Garden City and live out what few years they had left in idleness. They had to live frugally, but their hard working days were over. All they had to do was sit, just sit, their hands thin and work worn and their faces marked with seams of hard work, years and years of it.

The two boys, William in his late teens and Lemual in his early twenties, were out of a home. Lemual said goodbye to his parents and brother, stepped into the old A-fork saddle on the bay mare, and headed west. He carried a Colt .44 six-shooter, two blankets for a bed, three-days supply of dried beef and bread, and four gold dollars. Nothing more.

William, making his way to Kansas City, worked eight to ten hours a day in a factory and went to school nights. He finished the twelfth grade and kept on studying. He had his eye on medical school, and finally the time came to apply for admission.

'Don't try it,' the dean had said. 'No one without family money can manage it in medical school. You have to study fourteen hours a day, and no one can keep up with the studies and earn a living at the same time. I admire your ambition, young man, but...'

Teaching. There was a shortage of school teachers. Go back to Garden City and teach. It was a living and he could keep an eye on his folks. That's what he did.

Then came the letter.

Turner unfolded the letter and read it again. Lemual was happy. He and his partner had 'struck a vein,' he said in his letter, and uncountable wealth lay ahead. The partners had it staked and filed with the district recorder, 'and no one can take it away from us now,' Lemual wrote. To get to the claim, take the road to Canon City for two miles and go over a rocky hill to the west of the road. The partners' claim and their camp was just over the hill, between it and a creek.

'I hope you can come, Bill, because we could use another strong back and I know you'll leave here rich.'

It was summer, and Turner had decided he would go to Cripple Creek. If Lemual's exuberance faded and the vein was not what he thought it was, well, not much would be lost.

Then came the telegram.

It followed the letter by two days and it was from a deputy sheriff in El Paso County, Colorado. It said Lemual was dead. That was all it said.

Lemual, the wild one. Lemual who loved to ride a horse at a dead run and fire a six-gun at tin cans. Who loved to shoot at running jackrabbits on the Kansas plains with a six-gun. Who often persuaded his younger brother, William, to participate in the same sport. After all, it was said that ten jackrabbits ate as much grass as a cow, and the Turners had no pasture to spare. William was almost as good with a gun as Lemual.

But Lemual was no troublemaker. A man had to be tough to live on the Kansas frontier, and the two brothers got into their share of scraps. But Lemual was no troublemaker.

The child started crying again. The young mother rocked him and cooed to him trying to quiet him down. 'I'm sorry,' she said to Turner. 'I know some people hate to hear a baby cry. I'm sorry.'

'Where does your husband live, ma'am?'

'In Cripple Creek. But since there's no train going there, he said he'd meet me here.'

'What will you do if he doesn't show up?'

'I don't know. Try to find him. Ask the police.'

17

'There's a deputy sheriff in Cripple Creek. I'm going there on the stage in the morning. If your husband doesn't show up tonight, maybe you'd better go there too. You can find out what happened to him and you can have your child cared for by a doctor.'

The woman sighed wearily. Turner took off his thin, short coat, folded it and laid it on the seat beside her. 'Why don't you lie down? Use this for a pillow. I'll hold the boy.'

Weariness forced the woman to accept.

*   *   *

Six horses, almost matched, pulled the Hanley Stage Company's concord over the rocky road to Cripple Creek. Five passengers sat inside. They were Turner, Mrs. Mahoney and child, the bearded overall-clad gent and another man who was dressed the same way and wore the same type of beard. The concord bounced and swayed on its big springs, but in spite of that the child slept. The two bearded men talked about the gold that had to be 'just layin' thar waitin' for some mother's son to find it. Thar's goin' to be a lot of men git

18

rich outa that gold,' one of them allowed, 'and I aim to be one of 'em.'

'Me too,' said the former train passenger. 'But I got robbed of my stake and now I got to find a job.'

'First thing I'm gonna git,' said the other, 'is some grub and some prospectin' tools. Then I'm gonna git me a Winchester and a pocket full of cartridges. There's bushwhackers in these hills that'd cut a man's throat for a nickel.'

The stage climbed, dropped downhill, climbed again, then dropped into the huge bowl that held the town of Cripple Creek. The Sangre de Cristo Mountains stuck up on the horizon far to the west.

The driver pulled back on the six lines, pushed the brake forward with his foot and stopped the team in front of the Bluebird Hotel. 'Whoooe,' he said. 'Everybody off. This is whar I unload.'

A portly man wearing a star on his shirt pocket and a pistol on his hip stepped forward to watch the passengers unload. He had a cowboy hat pulled down to his shaggy eyebrows and a moustache that turned down at the corners of his mouth. He squinted at Turner, then turned his attention to the woman and child. 'I'm

19

Deputy Sheriff Lon Mitchell, ma'am. Is somebody meetin' you?' He talked with a southwestern drawl.

She spoke softly in a well-modulated but worried voice. 'I'm looking for my husband. Mike Mahoney. He was supposed to meet me at the train depot in Florissant.'

'What did you say your husband's name was?' The deputy corrected himself immediately, 'Is.'

Her face turned whiter. 'Mahoney. Is something wrong? Did something happen to my husband?'

The deputy looked down at his polished, calfskin boots, shuffled his feet and cleared his throat. 'I'm sure sorry to have to tell you this, ma'am. A man named Mike Mahoney was shot four days ago. Him and his partner. They're both dead. I'm sure sorry.'

The woman staggered back a step and Turner reached for her. Her knees buckled, but with Turner's help she stayed on her feet. Turner took the child out of her arms.

'You a friend of hers?' the deputy asked.

'Yes. I'd like to help her.'

'Best get her inside. Get her a room so

she can lay down.'

'I will. And Mr. Mitchell, I need to see you as soon as I can. My name's Turner. William Turner.'

Deputy Mitchell squinted closer at Turner, then said, 'I'll be in my office. Down the street.'

It was late summer and Bennett Avenue was crowded. There were men in flat-heeled jackboots and overalls, and other men in the laced boots and green corduroys that was the universal uniform of mining experts. Carbon arc lights on high poles looked down on freight wagons pulled by fourups and sixups.

Turner had promised Mrs. Mahoney he would find the doctor and send him immediately to her hotel room. That was his first chore. Then he had to find out what he could about his brother's death and also about Mike Mahoney's death. He went out on the street, looking for the doctor.

He stopped the first man he saw, a lean-jawed man wearing baggy wool trousers held up by a tight belt that seemed to squeeze him in the middle, and asked where he could find the doctor.

'Down to Canon City,' the man said.

'But I—we were told there is a doctor

21

here.'

'Was. Ain't no more. Packed up day before yestiddy and went back to where he came from.'

Turner couldn't believe it. 'Why? Do you mean there is no doctor here at all?'

'Nope. His office is down in the next block, but he ain't there. He's gone.'

'There's no one else?'

'Wal, there's Rose. She patched up a friend of mine once. Did a purty good job of it too.'

'Rose?'

'Over on Myers Avenue.' The man pointed to the east. 'In that red brick house over there.'

Turner went to the building and found Rose Vandel in a well-lighted parlor with red velvet wall coverings and lacy curtains. She was in the company of several other well painted young women.

'I'm not a nurse, but I've had some nurse's training,' she said. 'I hate to leave my business here this time of evening. It's about time for the shift change at the mill, and these girls have to be supervised. But, well, okay, I'll go and see if I can do anything.'

Turner couldn't help glancing around

22

the room at the other young women. Their smiles made him nervous. 'We would certainly appreciate it, Miss Vandel. We were told there is a doctor in town, but now I'm told he left.'

'Yes,' she said. 'The town's water system isn't the best and the last time he turned the spigot and got no water, he packed up and took the next stage to Canon City. I wish he'd stayed,' she added wistfully. 'Somebody's always getting hurt and I can't take the place of a doctor.'

Turner told her where to find the new widow and child, and got her to promise that she would go over there right away. Then he went back to Bennett Avenue, the main business street.

His white shirt, necktie and low-cut shoes attracted a few glances but not many. He walked past The New Gold District Bank and realized that he was not the only man dressed that way. Employees in the bank also wore white collars and neckties.

The deputy sheriff's office was not hard to find. An overhead sign stuck out over the boardwalk, proclaiming that here was the office of El Paso County Deputy Sheriff L. O. Mitchell. It said the county jail was in the same stone building.

23

The sun had gone down and Deputy Mitchell was lighting a kerosene lamp when Turner walked through the open door. A tall man, almost as tall as Turner, sat at the deputy's desk. He too was wearing a white shirt and necktie. He stood up as Turner walked in and stuck out his hand. 'You must be William Turner.'

'Yes I am. Did you know my brother, Lemual Turner?'

'I certainly did and it was a pleasure to do business with him and his partner. I was saddened to hear of their deaths, and I told Deputy Mitchell here to leave no stone unturned in finding out who robbed and murdered them.'

'Murdered?' Turner stopped dead still. 'The telegram didn't say he was murdered. And robbed?'

Deputy Mitchell blew out the match he was holding. 'Well, now, I sent a short message down to Colorado City to put on the Western Union wire. The gentleman I sent it with ain't got too good a memory and he don't read too good so I kept it short.'

'Was it murder?' Turner asked.

'Well, yes, they were shot in the back and robbed. I sent word to the sheriff down

24

to the county seat and he sent word back to just do the best I can. But don't worry, I'll find out who done it.'

Feeling suddenly weak, Turner sat in a wooden chair opposite the deputy's desk. He stared at the floor.

'We're awfully sorry about it,' the tall man said.

'We got their stuff, all but their tent, over here in the corner,' said Deputy Mitchell. 'That warbag and satchel 'pears to be Lem Turner's.'

Turner raised his head. 'Are you the mayor?' he asked of the tall man.

'Oh, no no no. I'm George Kemp. I'm president of The New Gold District Bank. I bought your brother's claim.'

'He sold his claim?'

'He surely did. Said he and his partner didn't have the funds to open a mine and it was easier to just sell.' The banker shook his head sadly. 'They didn't even get to enjoy the proceeds of the sale. Someone must have seen them leave my office with twenty thousand brand new dollars in their pockets.'

'Where did the murders happen?'

'At their claim,' the deputy sheriff answered. 'They went back to take down their tent and pack up. Somebody shot them clean through the heart from the back.'

'Where are the bodies?'

'At the Pisgah graveyard. We got no undertaker here and we couldn't keep the bodies very long. Wish we could have.'

'Are you sure it was my brother?'

'No doubt about it. Several men knew him and his partner, and he carried papers with his name on 'em. And we found a letter in his warbag with your name and town on it. That's why I sent you a wire.'

Turner was pensive a moment. 'Who was my brother's partner?'

'Why, didn't you know? It was Mike Mahoney. That lady's husband.'

CHAPTER THREE

The child had stopped crying when Turner knocked on the hotel room door. A white-faced Mrs. Mahoney admitted him and pointed to the child, covered to his chin on the bed. 'I'm afraid he's—he's dying,' Mrs. Mahoney sobbed uncontrollably.

Rose Vandel was bending over the boy.

26

She put her hand on his forehead. 'He's getting cold,' she said in a weak voice. She pushed back the eyelids, then pulled the blanket down and put her ear to the child's chest. Then Rose Vandel sobbed. 'I'm sorry. I couldn't save him.'

Mrs. Mahoney dropped to her knees beside the bed and buried her face in the blanket beside her dead son. Her sobs turned to silent, hopeless crying.

'What can we do?' Turner asked desperately. 'Can we do anything? Can you tell me what to do?'

He walked back and forth beside the bed. He wanted to touch the grieving woman, talk to her. He didn't know what to do. He turned to Rose Vandel. 'Can't we do something?'

'No.' Rose Vandel wiped her eyes with a perfumed handkerchief and blew her nose. 'There's nothing. Anyway, there's nothing you can do. Why don't you leave now. I'll stay with her. She needs a woman friend.'

'But your business.'

'Never mind my business. A woman's got to be good for something else.'

Deputy Sheriff Mitchell was sad when Turner told him about it. He pulled at the corner of his moustache. 'There's a woman that's had more than her share,' he said. 'Her husband gettin' killed and now her baby boy dyin'. And she's all alone in a strange town. Wonder if she's got any money?'

'I don't know,' Turner said. 'I'll give her some of what I've got if she needs it. I can work and earn my way back to Kansas if I have to. If I'm not mistaken,' he added, 'she came from a good family. She has an educated voice. But you know, I don't even know where she came from. She was on the train when I got on at Garden City.'

Another man wearing a star on his shirt entered the office then, and Deputy Sheriff Mitchell introduced him as a miner who helped keep the peace whenever the regular full-time deputy needed help. The man wore a miner's cap, flat-heeled boots, and sported a moustache that hid his upper lip. He nodded at Turner but said nothing.

'She didn't talk much, huh?' Deputy Sheriff Mitchell asked.

'Not much. She's proud. She never asked for help.'

Turner went through the heavy canvas duffel bag first, the bag that Mitchell called a warbag. All he found were two pairs of denim Levi's, a wool shirt and two pairs of

28

socks, both dirty. He opened the satchel next, and the first thing he saw was the old Colt .44 that his brother had owned since he was a teenager.

The pistol was fitted into a handmade cowhide holster. Turner could remember his brother making the holster, throwing away the first attempt and trying again. He remembered how Lemual had covered the gun with axle grease and had wet the holster thoroughly before putting the gun in it and letting it dry. When it was dry, the gun fitted into it perfectly.

It was early morning. The sun had just then climbed over the mountains to the east. Deputy Mitchell shivered aloud and started putting kindling into the stove.

'This's the coldest damn country I ever saw,' he said. 'It'd freeze the tail off a brass monkey. I swear I'm goin' back to Texas. Tell yuh, son, I wouldn't spend another winter here if they gave me a gold mine.'

The wooden stock of the .44 had been replaced with a hand carved one, but it felt familiar to Turner. He recalled firing many rounds with it at running jackrabbits. He checked the cylinder and found it fully loaded. Deputy Mitchell watched Turner fondle the gun.

'It's an old timer,' the deputy said, 'but it's been taken care of.'

'My brother traded a calf for it,' Turner said, 'and after he'd had it awhile he wouldn't have traded it back for a full-grown steer.'

The deputy chuckled. 'I never saw him use it, but I had a hunch he could have if he'd wanted to.'

There was no humor in Turner. 'Lem was no troublemaker. I'd like to find out who murdered him.'

*   *   *

The horse Turner rented was gentle and slow. He had to whip the animal lightly with the end of the bridle reins to get him into a trot. I don't blame him, Turner thought. He's been roughhandled and ridden half to death by so many men who patronize livery stables that he had to develop a stubborn streak out of self-preservation.

'Come on, old feller, I won't be hard on you,' Turner said aloud.

He rode first to the Mount Pisgah Cemetery and stood over the graves of his brother and Mike Mahoney. Only hand-

30

sawed wooden crosses decorated the graves. Someone had carved their names on a wooden marker at the head of each grave.

Turner stood a moment, head bowed. The shock that had come to him when he received the telegram returned. It was hard to believe Lem was dead. Lem, his older brother who had fought off the older bullies in school but told Turner he would have to do his own fighting when it came to kids his own age. Lem, who had saddled the bay mare and ridden off west, vowing he would make a better life for himself than his parents had ever had.

He would have done it too if he had lived, Turner allowed. Twenty thousand dollars for a claim in an area where hundreds of thousands of dollars worth of gold was being discovered? That's hard to believe, he said to himself.

He climbed into the saddle again and headed down the road toward Canon City. The boulder-strewn hill that Lem had described in his letter was easy to find, and Turner reined the rented horse off the road. It was a hard climb up the hill and Turner stopped the horse two-thirds of the way up to let him blow, then flicked the reins at the animal's rump to get him going again. He topped the hill between two boulders as big as the horse and immediately saw the tent. It was near a long strip of willow bushes which mostly hid a creek, just as Lem had said, and there was a deep hole in the ground a few yards ahead of it.

The horse stepped gingerly going downhill, and Turner stopped, dismounted and picked up the left front foot. Sure enough, the steel shoe was worn to paper thinness, and Turner silently swore at the stable owner who took no better care of his horses.

Horses were seldom shod in Kansas, but even a Kansan knew that a barefooted horse couldn't go far in the Rocky Mountains. And Turner knew that a horse's front feet took more punishment going downhill than on level ground. He led the animal the rest of the way down the hill.

The hole was about ten feet deep, and a ladder made of sections of aspen trunks stuck up out of it. Turner counted two other prospectors' holes nearby. He wouldn't have recognized gold if he had seen it, but Turner surmised that the deepest hole had to be where Lemual and

Mike Mahoney struck the vein.

He turned away from the hole and went into the tent. A thin, steel sheepherder's stove stood in the center with a few pieces of split firewood scattered around it. A few cans of groceries were stacked inside a wooden box beside two tin plates and a few forks and knives.

A tin washbasin was turned upside down in a corner of the tent, and along the far wall were two canvas cots covered with ragged blankets.

Outside again, Turner found digging tools behind the tent, and another wooden box that had once contained sticks of blasting powder. Among the tools were a hand drill, resembling a long chisel, and a sledge hammer to drive it between the rocks. Prospecting was hard work, Turner realized.

He looked around further and saw that the men had had to carry water a good one hundred yards from the small creek that was almost hidden in a forest of willow bushes. Aspen trees, with their pale trunks and shimmering leaves, were everywhere. A few of the leaves had already started turning yellow. Fall came early at that altitude, Turner suspected.

The horse, tied to a tree, whinnied in a short low gasp, and Turner saw that its head and ears were pointed uphill. Two riders were coming. Turner remembered that two men had been murdered there a few days earlier, and a cold knot formed in his stomach. But the riders, when they got close enough, turned out to be Deputy Mitchell and the banker, George Kemp.

Their horses were well shod and were half walking and half sliding down the hill. The banker bounced around in his saddle uncomfortably, but the deputy sheriff sat his horse as easily as he sat in his office chair.

'Mornin' again, son,' the deputy said as he reined up. He glanced skyward. 'Sure glad to see that sun up and warmin' things up.'

The banker looked hard at Turner. 'You're trespassing, you know. This property belongs to me now.' Gone was the affable, sympathetic attitude he had displayed in the deputy sheriff's office.

The change in attitude put Turner on the defensive. 'I just thought I'd look around,' he said, half apologetically. 'See what a vein of gold looks like. By the way, did you buy this tent and tools too?'

34

'No. I suppose you have a right to that. But this claim, this mine, belongs to me.'

'You plannin' on doin' a little prospectin' yourself, maybe?' the deputy sheriff asked.

'No. No, I don't know anything about looking for gold. I just thought I'd like to see the place where my brother was murdered. Mind telling me where you found the bodies?'

The lawman dismounted, but the banker stayed on his horse. Mitchell walked bowlegged to the far side of the tent. 'About here. I figure the shooter was in them willers over there.' He pointed toward the creek. 'He must've seen George here pay the men off and follered 'em. He sure cleaned out their pockets.'

'Are you sure there was only one killer?'

'Found two forty-four forty shell casings over there. Looked like they was both fired by the same Winchester. The firin' pin hit 'em both in exactly the same place.'

Turner puzzled that one over in his mind a moment. 'Both were shot in the back, you say?'

'Yup. We left the bodies in a shack behind my office a couple of days, and everybody that saw 'em would tell you the same thing.'

'Did you dig the slugs out?'

'Why, no. I'm no surgeon and the slugs would no doubt be so beat up you couldn't tell anything about 'em anyway.' The lawman squinted at Turner. 'Why?'

Turner shrugged. 'I don't know. I guess I'm just grabbing at any information I can get. I would like very much to see the killer arrested and brought to trial.'

The banker had been silent for a time, but he spoke up hastily, 'So would we, wouldn't we, Mr. Mitchell?'

'Sure would, son. Like I said, I'm figgerin' on goin' back south to Texas before the snow flies around here, and I'd like to get this cleared up.'

He bowlegged his way back to where his mount was ground tied, and picked up the reins. 'And I'll tell you, if we ever find out for sure who killed your brother and his partner, we'll hang 'em. Our trials around here are short and to the point.'

He swung into the saddle effortlessly. 'I'm goin' back to town. The best way to solve a killin' is to hang around town. Keep your eyes open and sooner or later somebody'll say somethin'. Then you start askin' questions.'

Turner turned toward the banker.

'Didn't you want something here?'

George Kemp snorted. 'I can't see that that is any of your business. And let me remind you again. You're on private property.'

CHAPTER FOUR

The two men rode away, their horses scrambling up the hill. Turner watched them leave. His rented horse also watched them leave, dancing around on the end of the bridle reins, wishing he could follow. After they topped the hill and disappeared, Turner walked around the tent, studying the ground. He found nothing interesting. He walked over to the willows and poked his way through them.

A rider could have come from the other side of the creek, he guessed, but if he had stayed out of sight he would have had to cross the creek far upstream, around a bend.

Turner went back to his rented horse, mounted and rode upstream toward town. What he was looking for, he didn't know. Perhaps to see where the creek came from.

He crossed the creek at a place where the willows were not so dense and found he could go no farther in that direction. A steep hill rose out of the creek on that side. It was the same rocky, pine covered hill that rose near the creek opposite the tent, but it was steeper upstream. It was almost perpendicular. No horse would climb it there.

Holding his hand in front of his face to ward off willow branches, Turner rode back across the creek and went on upstream. He had to ride across the foot of a gentler slope on that side of the creek to keep going upstream, and once on the other side of it, he could see that the creek meandered toward town. He reined the horse to a stop and sat there, thinking.

The bushwacker didn't follow the creek because he would have been in plain sight once he crossed the foot of the gentle hill. He couldn't have ridden in the willows because they were so thick nobody could ride a horse very far in them. And he couldn't have come from the other side of the creek because of the cliff.

Lemual would almost certainly have seen him approaching, Turner believed, because Lemual was well aware of the dangers of being robbed. And with twenty thousand dollars in their pockets, the two partners would have been watching.

No, the only way a bushwhacker could get within rifle shot of the tent was to dismount, leave his horse five hundred yards away on the other side of the gentle hill, and walk, even crawl, the rest of the way through the willows.

'I wonder if that's what happened,' Turner said aloud to the horse he was riding. The horse cocked one ear back at him. But would a robber leave his horse behind and walk and crawl a good five hundred yards through the dense brush, knowing that if he made a sound and was discovered, he could be shot? Well, Turner surmised, for twenty thousand dollars, I guess there are plenty of men who would.

Turner looked for horse tracks near the aspens and other places a horse could be tied on the opposite side of the hill. He found none. Whether that was significant, he didn't know. Rain can wash away tracks, he knew, and he guessed it rained often in the mountains.

And thinking of horses brought up another question. Lemual and his partner would have had horses. What became of them? That was a question the deputy sheriff could answer. If he knew anything at all.

Turner rode on upstream. He knew he was headed in the general direction of the town, and sure enough, after several miles, the creek crossed under a wooden bridge at the Canon City road. It was a longer route to town, Turner discovered, but it was another route. With a little blasting and scraping, a wagon road could be built along the creek. It was the long way, but it could be made passable.

No wonder Lemual and Mike Mahoney were willing to sell. It would take capital to build a wagon road to the mine, and it would take money to buy mining machinery. And it would take wagons and horses to get the ore to the mill. Selling was probably the easiest thing to do, all right.

But for twenty thousand dollars?

Rose Vandel was still sitting with Mrs. Mahoney when Turner got back to the Bluebird Hotel. Mrs. Mahoney was sleeping. 'I finally got her to lie down,' Rose Vandel said. 'She's a little better, but she's taking it awfully hard.'

'Is there anything I can do? Does she need money?'

'I think she has enough money. Her folks live in Kansas City, and I don't think they are poor. She's got an education. She said her husband just got bitten by the gold fever and believed he'd get rich around here. I get the feeling they weren't too well matched, but I'll bet she was loyal to him.'

'Kansas City, you say?'

'That's what she said. She wouldn't talk much at first, but finally she opened up. Poor girl.'

'Is there anything I can do? Can I talk to her?'

'Better not now. The funeral's tomorrow morning. The town hasn't got a place to keep dead bodies, and we have to bury them quick. She'll need a strong arm then. She'll need all the friends she can get.'

*   *   *

Turner recognized the bay mare immediately. She was older—had to be at least fifteen—but she was still stepping lively and proud. Seeing the horse brought back the memory of Lemual riding away, leaving home, going west, stopping just as he topped the hill on the west side of the barn, and waving goodbye. That was the

41

last time he had seen Lem. Now Lem was dead. Murdered.

The horse didn't recognize Turner, of course, but she came up and nuzzled his pockets and hands, looking for a tasty tidbit. 'You're looking good, old girl,' Turner said. He scratched the animal's neck and combed her mane with his fingers. Maggie, that's what Lem called her. The mare had more than earned her keep on the Turner homestead. She had pulled a plow, pulled a buggy, carried Lem and Bill on her back, raised a colt and even won a few short races. She had carried Lem west to, only she knows where now, and finally to Cripple Creek. 'You don't owe anyone anything,' Turner said aloud to the mare.

'Well, you owe four dollars board bill,' said the stableman. 'That is, if you want her.'

Turner paid the man. 'I'll have to board her here until I leave town. Then I can't take her with me. I'll give her to someone who will take good care of her. She's a good brood mare. Had a good colt once, and the colt won some races back in western Kansas.'

The stableman rolled a chew of tobacco

from one cheek to the other and spat a stream onto the ground. 'I know a rancher that'd like to have 'er. Got 'imself a thoroughbred stud and he's lookin' for some good mares. Probly pay a good price for 'er.'

'She was Lem's horse,' Turner said. 'I couldn't sell her. I'll give her to the man if he'll promise to take good care of her.'

'Oh, he'll take care of 'er. I never knew a man so much in love with horses.'

'What's his name?'

'Mr. Lancaster. Joel Lancaster. He's a good honest man and he's gettin' rich off the mines around here. Buyin' everything he can get that's got a speck of gold in it. Him and that banker, George Kemp, are seein' who can get the richest.'

'Tell him, when you see him, to take the mare. I'll sign a bill of sale if he wants.'

'Sure. Sure will. Say, what should I do with the other horse, that gray geldin' that belonged to your brother's partner?'

'It belongs to Mr. Mahoney's widow now. She'll probably want to sell him.'

'I'd give six dollars for 'im.' The stable-man looked away at the horizon, unleashed a brown stream, then looked back at Turner. 'Okay, ten dollars if you count the board bill.'

'I'll mention it to her,' Turner said.

It was midafternoon and Bennett Avenue was alive. There was a fever in the air. Gold fever. Men were getting rich from the gold mines, and many more were trying to get rich. New money was being spent lavishly, and fancy carriages pulled by matched teams of Morgans and Hackneys paraded down the street. Men yelled and waved across the street at each other. And the Spotted Pup saloon was doing a boisterous business.

The smell of food came out of the saloon as well as noise, and Turner remembered that he hadn't eaten since early morning. He followed the odor inside and discovered a lunch counter across the room from the bar. He had to stop a moment and admire the bar. It was of polished mahogany with a brass footrail at the bottom. The long mirror over the bar was framed by handcarved and polished walnut wood. The bartender, who was working rapidly with both hands, sported a long handlebar moustache, much like the one worn by Deputy Sheriff Mitchell.

Turner stepped up to the lunch counter and ordered a roast beef dinner with boiled potatoes and gravy. He sat on a stool and sipped a cup of hot, strong coffee while his meal was being prepared. He could feel the excitement himself, and he was made to understand how the fever can take hold of a man. Yes, this was the most exciting town he had ever been in.

The potatoes were not cooked done enough to suit Turner, but everything else was delicious. He ate every scrap, drained the coffee cup, and paid the short, fat man behind the counter.

'How was it?' the man asked.

Turner considered telling him about the potatoes, but quickly decided that complaining would serve no purpose. 'Very good,' he said.

'The spuds done?'

Turner managed a weak smile. 'Now that you mentioned it,' he shrugged.

'I was afraid of that,' said the cook. 'I boiled and boiled 'em. It ain't easy cookin' up here.'

Turner's face broke into a real smile. 'Yes, I guess this altitude would pose a problem for cooks up here where water boils at a comparatively cool temperature.'

'What?' The cook was puzzled.

'Never mind,' Turner smiled. 'I can see

45

what your problem is.'

He turned to leave and almost ran into a well dressed slender man who also had a smile on his face. 'Sorry,' said Turner.

'That's quite all right,' said the man. 'You must be Mr. William Turner.'

'Why, yes.' Turner looked the man over. He was dressed in a well tailored conservative suit with a pale blue shirt and dark blue tie. All that kept him from looking very much like a successful eastern stockbroker were his boots and hat. His pant legs were tucked inside cowboy boots which had obviously been worn where cattle walked. And his hat had the large curled brim of a rancher's hat.

He held out his hand. 'I'm Joel Lancaster. Old Jack at the livery stable described you. He said you want to sell that bay mare over there.'

They shook hands. 'I'm happy to meet you, Mr. Lancaster. The mare's not for sale. She's been in the family a long time. But if you want her for a brood mare and will see that she's well cared for the rest of her life, I'll give her to you.'

'It's a deal. I can get some good colts out of her. And don't you worry, Mr. Turner, no horse of mine is going to go hungry.'

'Would you like me to sign a bill of sale?'

'No. No, I don't happen to have one handy. Besides, if I say that mare is mine, no one is going to argue.' Lancaster's eyes crinkled at the corners.

Turner matched his smile. 'Yes, sir, I'll bet that's true, Mr. Lancaster.'

'You probably don't expect to be in town long, so I'll leave the mare at the stalls until you leave. That way you'll have a mount if you need one.'

'That will be fine, Mr. Lancaster.'

'Buy you a drink?'

'Thank you, but no, I haven't developed the taste for liquor.'

'I had a feeling you'd say that.' Lancaster offered his hand again. 'Good day, sir.'

The sun had set on top of the ridge to the west when Turner went out on the street again. He walked up one side of Bennett Avenue and down the other side, past the clapboard stores with false fronts, past the clothing stores and hardware stores with miners' and prospectors' tools in the windows, and past the saloons and cafes. The sun went down behind the horizon and reflected upward on the thin summer clouds that had gathered to the west. It turned them a bright red. In fact, Turner thought, it looked as if the horizon were on fire. Beautiful country, he said to himself. I can see why people fall in love with it.

He stepped into the street, then stepped back quickly as a heavy freight wagon rumbled past, pulled by four horses. The wagon was loaded with ore.

'Whar you goin'?' someone shouted.

'To the mill,' the driver answered. 'They're gonna squeeze a lot of gold outa these rocks.'

Turner crossed the street again and walked past the land recorder's wood-frame building, and noticed that the far end had been heavily damaged by fire. He stepped inside the open doorway and looked around. Workmen were just leaving, carrying their saws and hammers.

The far end had been gutted and was black with smoke damage. New wooden walls and partitions had been partially erected. Turner stepped aside to allow a workman to pass in the doorway. 'Sure burned things up,' he said, conversationally.

'Had a hell of a fire here for a little while,' the workman said. 'Lucky the whole buildin' didn't come down.'

'What started it?'

48

'Dunno. Probly some drunk sourdough droppin' his cigar. Looks like it started behind the recorder's desk though. The heat broke the windows on that side.'

The air had already started cooling down back on the street, and women on the boardwalks were hugging themselves to keep warm. A few men wore mackinaws. Turner went back to the Bluebird Hotel and climbed the stairs to his room. He found a wrinkled but clean shirt in his satchel, changed, poured some cold water from a tin pitcher into a tin pan and washed his face and hands. Then he went down the hall to Mrs. Mahoney's room.

She answered his knock and smiled weakly. 'I'm glad you came by, Mr. Turner. I need to talk to you. Won't you come in?'

Turner stepped inside and stood awkwardly. 'Please sit down,' she said, gesturing toward the only chair in the room. Turner sat.

'I, uh, I'm very sorry about everything that has happened, Mrs. Mahoney. I know it was a terrible blow.'

Her eyes were red rimmed, but her dark hair was combed and pinned neatly in a coil on the back of her head. She was wearing a dress that reached the floor and had a white, lacy collar. 'I appreciate your concern,' she said. 'And your help. I don't think I could stand it were it not for you and Miss Vandel.'

They were both silent a moment, wrapped in their own thoughts. Turner spoke next. 'I wished I could have saved him, Mrs. Mahoney. Your son, I mean. A doctor probably could have saved him. I, uh, had hopes of being a doctor one day, but I guess I was just pipe dreaming.'

Her face showed some interest. 'Did you, Mr. Turner?'

'Yes, I, uh, went to school in Kansas City, where I understand you came from, and I planned to go on to medical school, but I couldn't manage it financially.'

Her expression turned sympathetic. 'That's too bad. There will never be enough physicians.'

'A doctor probably could have saved your son. I wish I could have done something.'

She asked what he had learned about her husband's death, and he told her. She was already partially numb from shock and the news that her husband's death was murder had little effect on her.

'I'm not surprised,' she said, speaking calmly. 'Mike told me this was dangerous country.'

Turner told her about the gray gelding her husband had owned at the livery stables. He urged her to go to the hotel dining room and get something to eat.

CHAPTER FIVE

Supper was served in the dining room just off the main lobby of the Bluebird Hotel, and Turner accompanied Mrs. Mahoney there, pulled a chair out from a table, then pushed it gently under her. They both ordered steak, but she barely touched her food despite urging from Turner that she ought to eat to keep her strength up. Other restaurant patrons looked her way and sadly shook their heads. The words, 'poor woman,' reached the ears of Turner and Mrs. Mahoney more than once. The meal over, she went back to her room alone and Turner, feeling restless, went back outside.

The carbon arc lights were burning on four of the street corners, and light spilled out of store windows and saloon doorways. The air was fresh, and Turner wished he had a warm coat. Men were laughing inside the Spotted Pup, and Turner stopped a moment outside.

The laughter didn't help his glum mood. He couldn't get Mrs. Mahoney and her double tragedy off his mind. He also had Lemual on his mind, and the way Lemual had died. Suddenly he stood still. He heard something that sounded familiar. Something he had heard before. Something that brought back an unpleasant memory. What was it? He tried to get his memory working.

Laughter burst out of the Spotted Pup again, and then he remembered. One voice, one raucous laugh, could be heard above the others. It was the high whinny that had come from a masked man on a train. Surely, thought Turner, there aren't two men who laugh that way.

His jaw tightened and his pulse quickened. He had to know for sure. He stepped inside the saloon and looked carefully at the knot of roughly dressed men standing at the bar, joking with a painted, satin-sheathed Rose Vandel.

Turner studied the men carefully. Rose

52

Vandel said something funny and laughter rose out of their throats another time. Turner picked him out of the group. He was the right height and weight and had the same type of bushy eyebrows. He had changed boots and hats, but he was the man.

What to do? The man had a heavy pistol in a holster on his right hip and a skinning knife in a sheath on his left hip. Turner had no weapon. Go for the deputy sheriff, of course. That's the way it is done in a civilized society.

He walked rapidly down the street to the deputy's office. The door was locked and there was no light inside. He asked a passerby where he could find Deputy Sheriff Mitchell and was told the deputy lived in a cabin about a mile down the Canon City road.

He would have to walk or go to the livery stable, catch and saddle the bay mare and ride down. Either way, the robber would have time to be gone before the deputy could get back. Turner considered all possible actions, then reached a decision. That watch had belonged to his father and his father's father. He wanted it back. He pushed open the swinging doors and went inside.

Rose Vandel was the first to recognize him. She smiled a wide open smile and bellowed, 'Why Bill Turner, glad to see you out amongst us. How is Mrs. Mahoney?'

Turner said nothing. Jaws clamped shut, he walked up to the man who had robbed him. The man recognized him then. His smile quickly faded and his face went pale, then red. Turner stepped up close, his face only a few feet from the robber's face.

'You've got something of mine.'

'What?' the robber said. 'Who the hell are you? What the hell you talkin' about?' He stepped back a step.

Turner followed him, keeping close, watching his eyes. 'You know what. My wallet and my watch.'

'You're crazy. Who the hell are you?'

'I'm one of the men you and your partners robbed on the Midland train.'

A crowd gathered around the two men, sensing action.

The man's right hand went to his gun butt. Without thinking and reacting from instinct, Turner swung his right fist up from his waist. It connected squarely with the man's mouth. The man went down to a sitting position, grabbing for his gun as he fell.

A shot came from beside Turner and the robber's mouth sprung open. A red splotch appeared in the middle of his chest. He fell back, let out a loud sigh and died.

Two more shots sounded. They also came from beside Turner. Turner spun, ready to duck or run, he didn't know which. What he saw was Deputy Sheriff Mitchell with a gun in his hand, and two more men down on the floor.

Turner's gaze darted from one side of the room to the other, trying to figure out what had happened. The deputy sheriff spoke.

'Three on one ain't fair,' he said calmly. 'I thought I'd even the odds a little.'

Slowly, Turner let the tension drain out of him. 'What? Where did you come from?'

'I was down at the stable gettin' my horse when somebody came runnin' up and said he'd been robbed on the Midland train and the robbers was in here. I came arunnin.'

'It was me,' a familiar voice said, 'and them's the robbers.' It was the whiskered, overall-clad gent. 'Masks or no masks, I'd know 'em anywhere. I had a stake saved up and I want it back.'

'Do you recognize 'em too?' the deputy

sheriff asked Turner.

Turner pointed with his foot at the first man shot. 'If you'll look in their pockets, I believe you'll find some things that don't belong to them. I mean things they took off passengers on the Midland train.'

Another voice spoke up. 'Here's one you won't find.' It was the bartender, and he was holding up a gold watch. Turner's watch. 'He just sold it to me. I didn't know it was stolen. I paid a fair price for it.'

Deputy Mitchell went through the dead men's pockets and found two rings, a watch, folding money and the leather pouch taken from Turner's fellow passenger on the train.

'That's it, that's mine,' the whiskered gent exclaimed, reaching for it.

Deputy Sheriff Mitchell jerked the pouch back out of the man's reach. 'It ain't been properly identified yet.'

'I recognize it and the rings,' Turner said. 'I ought to, I was forced at gunpoint to collect them and drop them into a bag one of the robbers was holding.' He pointed with his foot again. 'I believe this one was the one with the pistol and the bag. He's the right size.'

Deputy Mitchell was pleased. 'Well,

looks like I just cleared up that train robbery,' he said to everyone present. 'You're sure about 'em?' he said to Turner.

'I'm positive about that one,' Turner pointed to the man he had hit. 'And I'm fairly certain about that one. They are the two who robbed the car I was in. I know there was another, but I didn't see him.'

'I did,' exclaimed the whiskered gent. 'I was lookin' out the winder and saw 'em puttin' on their masks. This is them. Now I want my poke back.'

'These are the ones,' the deputy said with finality. 'They were carryin' stolen rings and watches and money pokes. They've been identified. They would've been fools to keep the wallets. Probably threw 'em in a gully or somethin'.'

'I want my poke back.' The whiskered gent's voice was taking on a whining note.

'Not till it's identified so no questions can be asked,' the deputy said.

'Mr. Mitchell,' Turner said, looking the deputy squarely in the eye. 'It's his. I can identify it.'

The deputy hesitated, then with obvious reluctance handed the pouch to the whiskered gent. The man's face brightened inside the beard and he danced a little jig.

'Now, I'm goin' prospectin',' he declared.

Over the objection of the bartender, the lawman took Turner's watch, snapped open the back, squinted at the inscription and handed it to Turner. 'Says Jerome Turner on it. Must be yours. There's no other way to explain it.' He turned to the bartender. 'You'd better be more careful who you buy from, Jacob. A man that'd buy from a thief ain't much better'n a thief. Why'd you want a watch with somebody else's name on it anyway?'

The bartender grumbled, 'The gold in it is worth more than I had to pay.'

'You're not very smart, son,' the deputy said to Turner. 'Didn't you know old what's-his-name had friends? You told me yourself there was at least three of 'em robbed that train.'

Turner put the watch in his vest pocket. 'I wanted it back but I didn't mean for anyone to die. It wasn't worth killing anyone for.'

'Hell, I didn't kill anyone for a watch,' the deputy said. 'I killed 'em 'cause they was about to kill you. Hell, you might at least say thanks.'

'I do thank you, Mr. Mitchell.'

The deputy turned to the part-time

deputy who had just arrived. 'Help me get these corpses out of here and to the shed. See if you can find any papers with their names on 'em, and we'll send some more telegrams to the next of kin. If we can find any next of kin. Which I doubt.'

'By gawd, you must have done some mighty fast shootin', Mr. Mitchell,' the part-time deputy said. 'They didn't even get a round off.'

★ ★ ★

In his room at the Bluebird Hotel, Turner silently cursed himself. It was very foolish to confront a dangerous man that way without a weapon. It was just plain stupid.

Cripple Creek was a frontier town where men shoot first and ask questions later.

He opened his brother's satchel and took out the Colt .44. He checked the cylinder to make sure again that it was loaded, put it in the holster and strapped the holster around his waist. He drew the gun out rapidly several times to get the feel of it, then sat on the bed, thinking. Finally, he stood up, took off the gun harness and put it away again.

'No,' he said aloud. 'No, I will not be an

armed vengeance seeker. My goal is to be a doctor, to save lives, not take them. No, I will not go around armed.'

But after he undressed, blew out the lamp and crawled between the blankets, Turner had some more thoughts. In his mind he was not satisfied with the explanation of his brother's death. It could have been a bushwhacker after twenty thousand dollars, as the deputy sheriff said. But two men were shot in the back, supposedly from ambush. It was unlikely that both had their backs to the willows, the only place a bushwhacker could have hidden. And it was even more unlikely that both were shot at precisely the same time. One would have turned toward the sound of the first shot. One would have been hit somewhere other than in the back. Unless there were two bushwhackers and it just happened that both victims were looking away.

Turner didn't sleep much that night. His mind kept going back to the tent, two men shot in the back, a cranky banker, a fire in the recorder's building, and worst of all, a potentially valuable mining claim sold for twenty thousand dollars.

Lem wanted to be rich. That claim was

his chance. Would he have sold it?

Turner didn't sleep much that night.

*   *   *

For the second time in two days, Turner stood in the Mount Pisgah Cemetery, head bowed. The child was buried beside his father. The mother sobbed quietly, her shoulders shaking under the wool shawl Rose Vandel had given her. Only a half dozen people attended the burial. Rose Vandel put her arm around the mother and new widow, and talked softly to her. Turner stood beside her and wished he could find words that would help. A clergyman with a stiff white collar and black coat uttered a few words. 'This child and his family are not of our church,' he said, 'but it matters not. We are all God's children.'

He spoke quietly for a few moments, then walked over to the mother and stood in front of her as workmen began throwing dirt over the wooden box that had been built for a casket. When it was over, the clergyman helped Mrs. Mahoney into his buggy, drawn by one horse, and Turner was offered a ride in a light spring wagon driven by Joel Lancaster.

'I don't know the woman,' the miner-rancher said, 'but I thought somebody ought to go to the funeral.' He pushed the brake handle to the off position with his right foot and said, 'Giddy up,' to his two-horse team.

'It was thoughtful of you,' Turner said. 'It has to be terribly hard on the woman to lose both her husband and son within a few days and have to bury them in a strange land far away from her home. She could use some friends.'

'She looks and acts like a lady,' Lancaster said. 'Pretty too. I'll bet she's very pretty when she smiles. But I can understand why she wouldn't smile much these days.'

Back in town, Lancaster halted the team in front of a hardware store and got out of the wagon. 'Expect you'll be going back to Kansas now,' he said matter of factly.

'Oh, I don't know,' Turner said, climbing down. 'Not for a day or two anyway.'

'Is that right? You, uh, you aren't maybe looking to find out who killed your brother, are you?'

'I don't know,' Turner answered. 'I

would like to find out more about it all. I don't really know why, but I think I'll stay around awhile.'

'Take my advice, Mr. Turner, and don't go snooping around unarmed. There are some very dangerous men in this district, and a man's life isn't worth much.'

'I found that out last night. But I'm not ready to fight anyone to the death. I'll leave that up to the deputy sheriff. He seems to do that very well.'

'Don't depend on that deputy too much, Mr. Turner.'

'Why do you say that?'

'Now it's my turn to say I don't know. I do know he doesn't hesitate one second to kill. He's done it before. And there's something about him I don't trust. Sometimes he talks like a good fellow, a pretty decent sort. But he's a good politician. He sold the sheriff a bill of goods to get hired.'

Joel Lancaster looked at the horizon. 'I've met men like him before, Mr. Turner, and I'm sure you have too. You know, they talk like regular fellows, but they'll stab you in the back if there's anything in it for them.'

'Yes, Mr. Lancaster. I've met one or two

like that.'

*   *   *

The bay mare hadn't been ridden for over a week and she was pulling slack, wanting to run, as Turner headed her down the Canon City road. Well, why not, he said to himself. He pitched her the slack, and immediately the mare broke into a gallop, still pulling, wanting to run faster. 'Don't overdo it,' Turner said aloud. 'Take it easy and you'll go farther.'

It was a rough ride at first. Turner hadn't been on the horse for years. But soon the mare steadied down and galloped easily, and Turner began to get the feel of the saddle again. Then it became a pleasure.

The sky was a clear blue with only a few small puffs of clouds to the west, pure white clouds, looking like wads of cotton. The breeze fingered Turner's face and rumpled his hair, and it felt wonderful. He slowed the mare to a fast walk and looked around. He had never seen a sky that blue anywhere else, nor clouds that white. Way off to the west he could see the Sangre de Cristos, still covered in places with snow. The creek which ran parallel with the road in places was hidden by willows, and a wide strip on either side of the willows was covered with bushy cinquefoil and its thousands of tiny yellow flowers.

He rode past a one-room cabin with two corrals and a three-sided shed made of logs. They sat under a steep hill across the creek from the road. He surmised that that was Deputy Sheriff Mitchell's place, and he knew he had surmised correctly when he saw the deputy ride a buckskin horse across a wooden bridge and turn toward him. The deputy hollered.

Turner reined up and waited for the lawman to reach him. 'You're out early,' the deputy said. 'I usually get to the office earlier, but I had some stock to move this morning.'

'Are you a rancher too?' Turner asked.

'Yep. Small scale though. I got a couple sections and a few old cows. When I came here, oh, about two years ago, I thought this was the best grass country I ever saw. Grass was stirrup high on these hills and waist high to a tall Indian along the creek bottoms.'

Deputy Mitchell held the reins between two fingers of his left hand and rolled a cigarette, bending low to lick the paper without moving his rein hand.

'What I didn't know,' he went on after striking a kitchen match on his saddle and lighting up, 'is that the growin' season here is too short. The grass only grows maybe three months out of the year. And it grows slow. Once it's cropped off, that's the end of it for a year.' He took a deep drag off the cigarette, blew smoke, and pulled his hat down in front to ward off the morning sunlight.

'You wouldn't believe it, son, but it takes s many acres to graze a cow and calf round here as it does on the Texas desert. And besides, you have to cut and stack grass to have feed in the winter.'

The deputy was obviously in a talking mood, and Turner, not wanting to be standoffish, tried to be conversational also. 'It does look like good grass,' he said, 'but you can sure tell where it's been grazed.'

'Yep. I'm goin' back to Texas soon's I can find a buyer for my place.' Deputy Mitchell lifted his reins and started to ride away. 'Got to get to my office.' He stopped the horse suddenly and looked back. 'You goin' anyplace in particular?'

'Just riding,' said Turner.

'Well, if you're goin' to your brother's

camp, you might run into some of Mr. Kemp's help. Give 'em plenty of room and don't ask any questions of 'em. They don't know anything.'

'I won't bother them,' Turner said.

Deputy Mitchell rode on toward town.

Turner reined the bay mare off the road and again followed the long route to the mining claim. 'Yes,' he said aloud, 'a road could be built along the creek on this side. That's no doubt where Mr. Kemp will build it.'

The mare picked her way among th rocks easily and seemed to be enjoying the outing. 'It didn't take you long to get used to this rugged country, did it, old girl,' Turner said. 'You never had to do this in Kansas.'

He rode over the foot of the gentle hill and on up the creek. When he saw the tent he saw the men.

CHAPTER SIX

They wore jackboots and wool shirts. Two of the three men had pistols on their hips and the other had a rifle nearby. When they

67

saw Turner, their hands went to the pistols and the other grabbed up his rifle.

Turner reined the mare to a stop. 'Hello,' he yelled. 'I'm harmless. I'm not armed.'

'What in hell do you want?' one of them shouted back.

'I just want to look around,' Turner answered. 'My brother was killed there.' He touched the mare's sides with his shoe heels and she stepped forward.

The men said nothing as he rode up and dismounted. 'I'd like to look around and make sure they got all my brother's belongings,' he said, 'and I understand the tent belonged to him and his partner.'

One of the men stepped up and squinted at Turner's face. 'You do look something like Lem Turner, all right. Except you don't look to be half the man he was. Bigger, maybe, but a bloomer button. Hell, you ain't even got no calluses on your hands.'

The man was husky, with wide shoulders and wide hips. He had a two-day growth of beard.

The other two laughed.

Turner was becoming more and more aware that his manner of dress, his bare head, white shirt and low-cut shoes, were out of place in the mountains. But he set his jaw and answered, 'There are many things needing to be done beside working with one's hands.'

'Yeah,' the first man sneered, 'I heard you was a schoolmarm. Haw, haw. You're the first schoolmarm I ever saw that didn't wear a petticoat. Bet you got panties on under them pants.'

Turner tried to ignore the insults. 'You talk as if you knew my brother. Do you know anything about his death?'

'The last time I saw Lem Turner he had a bullet hole right where he couldn't reach to scratch it.'

Another man guffawed. 'It didn't itch anyhow.'

The big man stepped closer to Turner. 'You got no business here. You're trespassin'. Mr. Kemp told us not to let anybody come snoopin' around. Get on your horse and git before I take a notion to give you a whuppin'.'

Turner nodded toward the tent. 'That tent is now my property, and I intend to take it down and take it back to town.'

The big man stood spraddle-legged, hands balled into fists. 'Try it,' he said.

Turner took a step toward the tent and the big man was upon him, swinging big hard fists.

A blow glanced off the side of Turner's head, another landed in the middle of his chest, causing him to gasp for breath, and still another landed against his cheek, knocking him to his knees.

'Come on, get up, schoolmarm,' the big man sneered.

Turner stayed on his knees a moment, trying to clear his head. Then he came up fighting. He hadn't been in a fight since he was a kid, and his punches were awkward at first. But the big man was forced back, warding off the blows with his forearms. Suddenly it was like schoolyard brawls to Turner, and he remembered how to keep one hand punching and the other in front of his face for protection.

He jabbed straight out with his left hand repeatedly, stalking forward at the same time. Two of the punches connected, one solidly, and the big man was hurt. But he wasn't down, and he lowered his head and charged, fists swingly wildly. Turner remembered what to do. He coolly stepped back, watched for an opening, then swung his right fist up from his knees.

He heard a satisfying smack and a shock went up his arm as the blow caught the big man solidly in the mouth. The man went down.

Then Turner was grabbed from behind. One man had him in a bear hug and another, a short man, was hitting him in the stomach and head.

His knees sagged and he wanted to fall, to cover up his head. The man behind him held him up while the second continued to pummel him. He wrapped his arms around his face and was pounded in the stomach. He dropped his hands and was hit repeatedly in the face.

Finally, they released their hold and he fell onto his hands and knees. He was kicked brutally in the side of the face, and he blacked out.

The bay mare was cropping the grass nearby when consciousness returned. She stepped on the reins, but wisely picked up her feet one at a time until she was free again. Turner crawled to his knees and fell back onto the seat of his pants. He was squinting through one eye. The other was swollen shut. He got slowly to his feet, staggered a few steps and fell onto his knees again. He got up a second time and stood swaying, squinting.

The horse was happily going after the tall mountain grass.

Turner took two more steps and felt a sharp pain in his left side. His head felt as if it was going to explode. He took two more steps and was surprised to find himself still standing. He squinted around. The men were gone. He walked, slowly, painfully, to the creek, knelt beside it and splashed water onto his face.

Eventually, his head cleared. He could still see with only one eye, but he could see. He sat on the cool ground and stayed there a full twenty minutes.

The old horse stood perfectly still as Turner pulled himself into the saddle, then stepped out gently when he squeezed her sides with his legs. 'If there was ever a time when you want to take it slow, now is that time,' Turner said. The horse seemed to understand as they headed for town.

'My gawd, what happened to you?' the stableman asked. Turner told him he fell off his horse. 'Need some help gettin' back to wherever you're stayin'?' the stableman asked.

'No. I can walk. Thanks anyway.'

His stomach muscles were on fire, and

his head throbbed. Turner walked the one and a half blocks to the Bluebird Hotel. He kept his head down as he walked through the lobby, hoping his wounds would not be noticed. Finally in his room, he pulled off his shoes and collapsed on the bed. After awhile, the pain subsided a little and he slept.

Through the fog he heard a faint knocking on the door. It couldn't be. Get back to sleep, he told himself. The knocking persisted. 'Mr. Turner.' More knocking. 'Mr. Turner.' He forced his eyes open and sat up. It hurt to move.

'Mr. Turner.' More voices came from beyond the door. 'I'm afraid for him. Can you use your pass key?' It was a woman's voice. The door opened and the hotel clerk came in, followed by Mrs. Mahoney.

'Oh, you gave us a scare,' she said. 'They told me you appeared to be injured when you returned last evening, and I was worried.'

'I'm, uh, I'm all right,' Turner mumbled through swollen lips.

She let out a small gasp and stepped swiftly to his side. 'You are injured.'

She took off her borrowed shawl. 'I'll see what I can do. Lie back down, Mr. Turner,

73

and let me look at your wounds.'

'I'm, uh, I'm all right,' he said.

'No you're not. Just lie back, now.' She brushed the hair away from his forehead and studied his face, her face close to his. She had pretty brown eyes, Turner noticed.

The hotel clerk spoke. 'Is there anything I can do, ma'am?'

'I don't think so,' she said, 'unless we have to take him to a doctor somewhere. I may need some help moving him. Where is the nearest hospital? Colorado Springs?'

'Yes, ma'am. If you need some help, just say so.' He closed the door quietly behind him as he left.

'What on earth happened to you?'

'I, uh, fell off a horse.'

'Hogwash. You were beaten. No horse did this.'

'No, I—' His protest was weak.

She started unbuttoning his shirt. 'You can't fool me, Mr. Turner. I've seen beaten men before. My father is a physician in Kansas City, and I've had to help him patch up men who were caught in the labor wars.'

This was the widow Mahoney? The young woman who had just lost her

74

husband and son? Who was never seen smiling or doing anything but being helped? She was suddenly another person. She was taking charge and she knew what she was doing.

She probed his sides with her fingers. 'Does this hurt? This?' She pushed her fingers into the pit of his stomach, and he inhaled sharply. 'Uh huh,' she said.

'Fortunately, Mr. Turner, I don't believe any ribs are broken, although you certainly have some dandy bruises. Now let's see that eye.'

Gently, she pulled back his eyelid. He could smell the woman sweetness of her. She clucked like a mother to a son, then went to the washbasin and filled it with water from the tin pitcher. She soaked a towel, wrung it out, folded it and placed it over his eyes. 'I don't suppose there is a drugstore here either. I could use some things.'

His voice was stronger now. 'Are you by any chance a nurse, Mrs. Mahoney? You said your father is a doctor.'

'I'm not a nurse. I've had quite a bit of experience helping my father, but I've never had any formal nurse's training. My father is a very good teacher, however.'

75

She replaced the wet towel with a fresh one, and soon Turner felt better. He started talking then.

He told her again about his own ambition. How he had gone through a four-year college in Kansas City and had taken his pre-medical courses. He told her of his disappointment when he was not admitted to medical school for financial reasons. He told her about his folks, the old homestead, his brother.

She listened attentively.

He talked about himself more than he ever had before in his life, and suddenly he realized it. 'I'm sorry. I didn't mean to force my life history on you.'

She was all sympathy. 'I'm glad you did, Mr. Turner. You're a quiet man, and I've wondered about you. You are obviously a very ambitious and determined man, and I've a feeling you will get into medical school and become a very fine doctor. My father might be able to help. His family might be able to help. His family financed his education, but he has helped others who were not so fortunate. He'll help you too.'

Turner managed a weak smile. 'I could sure use some help.'

She went downstairs to the restaurant
76

and brought back some soup. Turner's jaws were too sore to eat anything more. She also brought a pitcher of milk and expressed pleasant surprise that Turner liked milk.

'I was afraid a big strong man like yourself would think it unbecoming to drink baby food,' she said, 'but my father always said milk is the most nearly perfect food in the world and nothing is better for the ill.'

Turner grinned crookedly. 'It'll never take the place of beefsteak. But I was brought up on a frontier farm and milk was one commodity we had plenty of.'

She kept cold compresses on his swollen eye, and soon he got up and walked around the room, trying his legs. She went back to her room and left him alone for awhile.

Turner couldn't get her out of his mind, the way she had changed from a weepy widow to a take-charge, knows-what-she's-doing type of woman. She must be one of those who don't show their strength until it is needed, Turner thought. And so pretty. Clear skin, slender figure and expressive brown eyes.

Sad eyes. Yes, the sadness was still there. One look at her eyes and one would know she had been hurt. It would take time to get over that. Yes, Turner thought, it will take time.

Thinking of Mrs. Mahoney's loss reminded Turner of his own family's loss. Lemual. His father and mother had taken it hard. They hadn't seen Lemual for five or six years, but they talked of him often, and his mother always looked sad when Lem's name came up in conversation. She had often remarked, 'I wonder where Lem is now. I wonder if he's well.' And a tear would run down her wrinkled, work-aged face.

'It's about Lem, Mother,' Turner had said. 'It, uh, he's—' he had begun to unfold the telegram.

'Lem's dead, ain't he?' his mother said matter of factly.

The old man had come into the living room of the three-room cabin in Garden City. 'What is it, Bill? Did something happen to Lem?'

Turner told them about the telegram from Deputy Sheriff Mitchell and the letter he had received from Lem just a couple of days earlier. He was barely able to keep his own voice from choking. The old couple sat together on the once-elegant, velvet-covered couch that she had inherited from her mother and cried silently.

The telegram was too brief, and it was agreed that William would take the next train to Colorado and see what he could find out.

And what had he found out?

All he knew was that Lem and a partner had done considerable prospecting and had finally struck a vein that looked promising. That a banker had persuaded them to sell, probably with the argument that it would take a considerable investment to mine the claim and haul the ore to a mill. That they had sold for ten thousand dollars each.

Twenty thousand dollars cash?

Why would the banker lie about that? And yet, would a banker have twenty thousand dollars cash he could hand out? Or would he have given them checks for that amount, checks they could cash at Colorado Springs or Colorado City? Wouldn't they have preferred checks to cash?

And with that much cash in their pockets, wouldn't they have been careful? Lem would have been. He had been on his own for years, often finding himself in a rough crowd. He had mentioned in a letter that a man's life isn't worth much on the frontier. He was no fool. He would have been careful.

Shot in the back. Both of them.

Turner was walking the floor in his sock feet. For awhile he forgot the sore muscles and the sore jaw. Murdered. And the killer or killers got twenty thousand dollars cash.

That is all Turner had been able to find out on his trip to Cripple Creek. But, by George, he had more questions to ask.

CHAPTER SEVEN

The banker was indignant when Turner asked him. 'Receipt? Why should I show you a receipt?'

'Listen, Mr. Kemp, I'm no lawyer, but it seems to me those men ought to have signed something when they turned their mining claim over to you.'

George Kemp stood up behind his desk in a small office just off the lobby of The New Gold District Bank. 'Of course they signed something. They signed the claim over to me. I filed it with the district recorder, where all claims are filed.'

80

'Why did you pay them in cash?'

'Because they wanted cash. Said they intended to do some more prospecting and wanted cash to buy supplies. With a check they would have had to go to Colorado City or Canon City to buy supplies.'

'I'm surprised a small bank like this one would have so much cash on hand.'

'Well, we don't advertise the fact, but yes, we can handle a cash transaction if necessary.' George Kemp added, as if it made a difference. 'It was new money. Just out of the mint.'

Turner was silent a moment.

'Does that answer your questions? Because if it doesn't, if you have any more questions, I just might tell you to get your answers from Deputy Sheriff Mitchell.'

George Kemp sat back down, angrily grabbed up a sheaf of papers and pretended to study them. 'Good day, sir,' he said gruffly.

The district recorder's building was just a block down the street, and workmen were still sawing and hammering, repairing the section of the interior that had been destroyed by fire.

The recorder, a middle-aged woman, began shaking her hand negatively before

Turner could finish his question.

'Right now, I couldn't prove who owns what,' she said. She waved an arm in the direction of the workmen. 'Some of my books were burned up.'

'How does anyone prove what they own?'

'Oh, not everything was burned up, and we haven't had any problems yet. Everybody around here knows who owns what and if anybody tried to claim somebody else's property, he'd have a battle on his hands. And I don't mean a legal battle. Besides,' the recorder smoothed down her long dress over wide hips, 'when they elected me recorder in the new Cripple Creek Gold Mining District, they trusted me, and I've got a pretty good head for money.'

'Listen, Mrs. uh—'

'Mrs. Hankins.'

'Thank you. Listen, Mrs. Hankins, my name is William Turner. I'm the brother of Lemual Turner who was murdered, you know?'

'Oh yes, I'm sorry.'

'What I'd like to find out is whether George Kemp can prove he bought a mining claim from my brother and his partner. Did he file anything with you?'

'He filed something. I was closing at the time, and didn't want to open my books, and I left it in my desk and promised I'd enter it in the books next morning.'

'He accepted that?'

'Sure, why not?'

'Is that a common practice?'

'No. But Mr. Kemp is an understanding man.' The recorder looked up at the ceiling a moment, thinking. 'In fact, I remember him insisting that I not bother with it that night. He said next morning would be fine.'

'Did you look at the paper he handed you?'

'I didn't read it, but I know it was a legal paper and it was notorized. I did see that much. And it had signatures on it.'

'But the fact is Mr. Kemp can't prove he owns that claim?'

'No, I guess not. Not by my books anyhow. But everyone knows he does. Those men, your brother and Mr. Mahoney, were seen in the bank, and Thelma Goodrow over at the bank witnessed their signatures. She's a notary. She put her seal on the paper.'

Turner was glum. What had looked for a

moment like a promising lead was not so promising after all. He thanked Mrs. Hankins.

'You're welcome, sir. What happened to your eye?'

'I fell off a horse.'

Deputy Sheriff Mitchell was sitting back in a chair with his booted feet resting on an upside-down wastepaper basket, reading a Dallas newspaper. 'It came on the stage yesterday,' he said. 'I get it by mail about once a week. Like to keep up with what's goin' on in Texas. Say, what happened to you?'

'Some of your citizens didn't like my trying to search my brother's tent and they pounded on me.'

The deputy's feet hit the floor and he stood up, pushing his hat back and allowing a thick sheaf of gray hair to escape from under the hat brim. 'When did that happen?'

'Yesterday.'

'And you're just now reportin' it to the law?'

'I didn't feel too good for awhile, to tell you the truth. All I wanted was to get back to the hotel.'

'Yeah, well, you took your time this

mornin'. I know you was in George Kemp's office over half an hour ago, and I seen you go into the recorder's shack.'

'Does George Kemp tell you everything?'

'Just about.'

'I had some business that couldn't wait.'

'What business?'

'Deputy Mitchell, there are some things I don't have to tell you about, and what I do at the bank and recorder's office are among them.'

'Oh, one of them I-know-my-rights kind of fellers, huh? Might have known. All right, tell me what they look like.'

Turner described the men. The deputy shook his head negatively. 'Don't remember seein' 'em around. And I'd probly of noticed 'em if they'd been around town long. Tell you what I'll do. I'll ask around, see if I can find out where they set up camp. Maybe my part-time helper has seen 'em.'

'All right, but in the meantime, Mr. Mitchell, I intend to search that tent. I'd take it down and bring it back to town if I had a way to transport it. It was my brother's tent, at least he had a half interest in it, and now it belongs to me and Mrs.

Mahoney.'

'What in hell you lookin' for?'

'Mr. Mitchell, I don't really know. I just want to look.'

The deputy squinted at him. 'You act like a man that suspicions somethin'. You better tell me about it.'

'I don't really suspect anything, Mr. Mitchell. All I know is my brother was murdered and the guilty party or parties are still at large. Of course, I'd like to see them brought to justice.'

'You hintin' that I'm not doin' my job?'

'No, Mr. Mitchell, not at all. There are thousands of unsolved crimes in this country, probably in this state, and you don't have much here to work with.'

The lawman sat down again, took off his hat and ran his fingers through his hair. 'I'm askin' questions every day, son. Now I cain't promise to find out who killed your brother, but I'm tryin'. And I don't think you'll do any better. In fact, you'll probly get yourself beat up again, the way you're goin' around accusin' people like George Kemp. And maybe you'll get yourself shot. Why don't you get on that stage and go on home? Leave the sheriffin' to me.'

Turner sat in a chair across from the

deputy's desk. 'I'm not accusing anyone of anything. I'm just curious, that's all. I'll probably leave in a couple of days and you won't see or hear from me again.'

'Tell you one thing, son. I'll breathe easier when you do leave. You're lookin' for trouble.'

Turner forced a grin. 'But in the meantime, I'd like another look at that tent.'

'All right. If you're afraid of gettin' beat up again, I'll get my horse and ride out there with you.'

Deputy Sheriff Mitchell's sorrel gelding was only half broken and acted as if he would buck if given a chance. The lawman sat his saddle easily, handling the horse with a light rein and seemingly paying no attention to him. 'Oh, he's a little snotty,' Mitchell said, 'but I'll tell you, son, if you want to get across country in a hurry, this ol' pony can sure stack the scenery behind 'im.'

It was another bright sunny day, and Turner said so.

'Sure, but don't let it fool you, son. In another month or so the snowballs'll be flyin'. That's when I shuck this badge and get myself back to El Paso. They say that's the hottest place this side of hell, and that makes it just right for me.'

Turner had to chuckle at that.

The tent was sagging but still standing when they rode up to it. They could see where fresh digging had taken place in the prospecter's hole started by Lemual Turner and Mike Mahoney. Broken rock was scattered around the hole.

'Wonder what kind of ore they found,' Deputy Mitchell said. 'I hear it ain't too good.'

'That's not what my brother said,' Turner replied. 'He was pretty excited about it. I'm thinking it was worth more than twenty thousand dollars.'

'It ain't worth a nickle till some ore is brought out and hauled to the mill,' the deputy said, 'and that takes capital.'

They dismounted and tied their horses close together to a tree. 'Hope that mare of yours ain't horsin',' the lawman said. 'I don't want my gelding kicked.'

'I've never known her to kick at anything,' Turner answered.

The two men went inside the tent. It appeared nothing had been disturbed. 'Satisfied?' the deputy asked. 'Nothin' to see here.'

'You're probably right,' Turner walked around, head down, looking at the dirt floor. He opened the sheepherder's stove and looked inside. He picked up the few sticks of split firewood and put them down. He looked at the ceiling.

'If I knew what you're lookin' for, I'd help you.'

'I don't know, Mr. Mitchell. Nothing in particular and everything in general.'

He walked outside, walked around the tent, studying the ground and the canvas walls. He went back inside and sat on one of the cots. 'I guess I'm just wasting your time. Mr. Mitchell. If you have anything else to do, why don't you go on back to town?'

'I'll stick around. See you don't get in any trouble again.'

Turner leaned back and studied the ceiling again. He turned on his side and saw the pencil marks on the wall next to the cot. He sat up with a start and squinted closer.

The marks were barely visible and had been made with a lead pencil. 'I wish I had more light,' Turner said.

'What'd you find, son? Anything interestin'?'

'I don't know. I can't read it. I need

some light.'

Turner got up, went to the front of the tent and folded the flaps back on top of the tent, letting in more sunlight. He pulled the cot away from the wall and sat on it, facing the markings, his face only inches away.

It was a column of figures with a few words: wagons 3, horses, 12, dynamite 100 pounds, pulley, cable. A line had been drawn under the column and under that was the figure $5,000.

The deputy sheriff was also squinting at the column of figures. 'Looks like somebody was doing some cipherin' on how much it would cost to work this claim, or build a road, or somethin'.'

'That appears to be it,' Turner said. 'Someone used the wall here instead of paper to work on.'

'Over here's some more,' the deputy said.

Two feet away from the column of figures was another figure, barely readible. It read: 20,000 X 4. The markings that followed were not discernible.

'Wonder what that means?' asked Mitchell.

'I wish I knew,' Turner said. 'It might

mean something important. And maybe it doesn't. I wish I knew.'

Turner searched every inch of the walls, hoping to find more pencil markings, but he found no more. What he did find was a burlap bag half full of rocks under one of the cots.

He opened the bag, took out one of the rocks and studied it. 'Must be gold ore,' he mused.

Mitchell reached into the bag and took out another rock. 'Yep, that's what it is. You can see a fleck of gold in it.'

'Guess I'll take it back to town,' Turner allowed.

'What for? Takes a lot more ore than that to be worth anything. The best mine around here only assayed out at a little over two hundred dollars a ton.'

Turner walked outside again. The deputy followed him.

'Mr. Mitchell, where do you think the ambusher fired from when my brother and his partner were shot?'

The deputy nodded toward the willows and the creek. 'Like I said, over there. No doubt about it. We found two empty forty-four forty cartridges over there.'

'And you already said the bullets were

not removed from the bodies to determine what caliber they were?'

'No. Who around here is gonna do that? Hell, son, I'm no undertaker. Cuttin' into dead men ain't somethin' I like to do before breakfast. Or any other time.'

'I see. You don't know for certain then that those empty cartridges were fired by the murderer?'

'Sure I'm sure. Those victims didn't have a forty-four forty or any kind of rifle. Why else would they be there?'

Turner stared at the deputy for a moment, thinking. 'I'll bet there are a hundred forty-four forty rifles in El Paso County.'

'At least. Ever since that caliber came out about eight-to-ten years ago, I've seen more of them than anything else. I'll stick with the old forty-five seventy U.S. Government cartridge myself.'

'Is there a ballistics expert in El Paso County?'

'I doubt it. Besides, what am I supposed to do, fire a bullet out of every Winchester forty-four forty around here and compare slugs? And what would I compare 'em with? Do you want to dig up those bodies and cut the slugs out of 'em?'

'No, I guess not. I was just thinking out loud, Mr. Mitchell.'

'I do that myself sometimes. But you've got a way of sayin' things that sound like you're accusin' somebody of somethin', like I wasn't doin' my job right.'

'I'm sorry, Mr. Mitchell. I'll try to keep my thoughts to myself.'

'I'll tell you again what you ought to do. You ought to quit thinkin' and get on back to that schoolhouse where you come from. Next time somebody points a gun at you I might not be around to shoot first.'

With that, the lawman stomped over to his horse and gathered the reins. Then, bronc-rider style, he grabbed a handful of the horse's mane in his rein hand and the saddle horn in the other, stuck his toe into the stirrup, shoved his knee against the horse's shoulder and swung up into the saddle.

'I'm goin back to town. I've got better things to do than be your bodyguard.' He touched spurs to the horse's sides and rode away at a gallop.

Bill Turner prowled around the tent, the creek, and the hole in the ground for another hour, then loaded the sack of ore onto the saddle in front of him and went back to town.

CHAPTER EIGHT

Mrs. Mahoney was a horsewoman. Turner could see that as she stepped into the saddle aboard the gray gelding her husband had owned. 'Oh yes, I've always been crazy about horses,' she said. 'I pestered the neighbors about their horses so much my father finally bought me a horse of my own. A thoroughbred.'

Bill Turner was riding the bay mare. They were going to the cemetery, and Turner carried a basketful of wild flowers that Mrs. Mahoney had picked on a hillside near town. There were flowers of every color and design.

She rode astraddle the horse, even though some women still thought that unladylike. She had bought a pair of rough denim pants and a plaid shirt to wear.

She looked around at the green hills, the mine dumps and mine headframes. 'Seems to be more of them every day,' she said, waving toward an open hole in the ground, surrounded by piles of low-grade ore that had been hauled out of the hole and dumped.

'Yes,' Turner said, 'quite a few people are getting rich here. Your husband and my brother probably would have become rich if they had not sold their claim.'

'Seems strange they would sell it,' she said. 'I mean, Mike wrote me every few days and all he could write about was how they had found one of the best veins in the area and they were soon going to be able to buy the whole town.'

'That banker said they didn't have the capital to work a mine,' Turner said. 'They would have had to build a road and one thing and another, and he said they sold to him for that reason.'

'I'm sure Mike had more in mind than twenty thousand dollars.'

'I think so too, Mrs. Mahoney.'

Her eyebrows arched. 'You do? Do you suspect something, Mr. Turner?'

'No. I mean, not really. I've been asking questions, but I haven't found out anything that would make me suspicious. It's just that it doesn't seem right.'

'I heard that the recorder's office burned down and no one can prove who owns some of the property here.'

'It didn't burn down, Mrs. Mahoney, just one end of it was destroyed. But it was the end where land records were kept. Not much was salvaged.'

'Oh.' She was silent a moment, then, 'Do you mean that that banker can't really prove he bought the claim from Mike and your brother?'

'He has witnesses,' Turner said. 'All kinds of people saw them in the bank with the banker, and a bank employee, who they say is an honest woman, witnessed and notorized their signatures.'

'Oh.'

'But doggone it,' Turner blurted out, then caught himself. 'Excuse me, Mrs. Mahoney.'

'Quite all right. I've heard men speak in exasperated tones before.'

'But doggone it, all they saw was a paper with signatures on it. Nobody can say what else was on that paper. Apparently they signed an agreement with the banker. And they are both dead and can't tell what they signed.'

'You do suspect something, don't you?'

Turner fingered the bay mare's mane. 'I have absolutely no proof of anything. But I'm going to stay here a few more days to try to find out.'

They rode in silence, both deep in their own thoughts. Mrs. Mahoney spoke next in a low, faltering voice. 'I'm staying too. My husband and my little boy are buried here. I can't leave them yet.'

★ ★ ★

'Mrs. Hankins,' asked Turner of the district recorder later that day, 'did you say you put the banker's notorized paper in your desk?'

'Yes, in the top right hand drawer.'

'Mind if I look?'

'You can look if you want to, but you'll have to go to the dump to find it. I have already searched the desk—what was left of it—and there isn't a piece of paper there that anyone can read.'

'Where is it, Mrs. Hankins?'

'At the dump. I saw them load all the trash and burned-up papers on a wagon. The dump is just south of town.'

Bill Turner found the remains of two desks. He suspected without opening them that he would find nothing in them, even though one of the desks wasn't completely destroyed. He climbed over trash at the

97

town dump and turned the destroyed desk right side up. The top right hand drawer was badly burned, but he was able to open it in one piece and sift through the papers in it. No paper was whole, but there were several with legible top halves or bottom halves that he was able to read.

He studied each paper carefully, often holding them up to the sun, trying to read the charred portions. None of them was the paper he was looking for. He did learn that he had the right desk. Several of the papers were business correspondence addressed to District Recorder Mary Ann Hankins. In fact, a handcarved wooden name plate still had the last four letters of her name. No use searching the other desk. This was the one the paper with Lem's signature had been put into. So much for that.

Turner figured the next person to see was Mrs. Goodrow, the woman who witnessed the sale of his brother's mine. He rode into town and knocked on her door.

'Yes, I'm Mrs. Goodrow.'

'Are you a notary public?' Turner asked.

'Yes I am.'

'My name is William Turner, Mrs. Goodrow. I'm the brother of Lemual Turner who was murdered.'

Her eyes widened, and she clucked sympathetically. 'Oh, I'm sorry about your brother. He seemed like a nice man.'

'Where did you meet him, Mrs. Goodrow?'

'In the bank.'

'Excuse my asking so many questions, ma'am, but I'm trying to learn more about my brother's death and his business. Would you mind telling me how you happened to meet him?'

'Why, I just notorized his signature, that's all. His and the other gentleman's, Mr. Mahoney's.'

'This is important, Mrs. Goodrow, did you see what sort of an agreement they signed?'

'No. I remember very clearly. Mr. Kemp had his hand over the top half of it. I did see the figure twenty thousand dollars, though.'

'You're sure? He held his hand over it so you couldn't see the top half?'

'Yes. That is, I remember he had his hand over the top of the paper, but I can't say he wanted to keep me from seeing it. The door was open and there was a little breeze in here. He was probably just holding the paper down on the desk.'

'Was there anyone else in the bank then? I mean people who might be capable of murder? You know what I mean, people who would see the men put the money in their pockets?'

She pondered the question carefully. 'There are always people in the bank. And—no, I don't remember anybody unusual. I remember several miners. And Deputy Sheriff Mitchell. And the clerk from the hotel. That woman, Rose Vandel, was there. And us employees. I don't remember anyone else.'

'Did you know the miners?'

'No. I think I've seen one or two of them in there before, but no, I didn't know them.'

'Thank you, Mrs. Goodrow.'

It was now midday and Turner went to the hotel's Bluebird Restaurant for a noon meal, hoping he would see Mrs. Mahoney there. He had left her at the hotel entrance when they returned from the cemetery, and took both their horses back to the stables. He was disappointed when he saw she was not there, but he knew he had no right to be disappointed. She couldn't be interested in him, or any other man.

The restaurant was crowded and Turner

had to sit at a table for two in a far corner. He had a long wait for the ground venison and boiled potatoes he ordered. The meal would have been tasty, but the butcher ground up some bone with the meat, and Turner, with his still-sore jaw, had to wince every time his teeth clamped down on a piece of bone.

Many voices created a steady hum inside the restaurant, but suddenly the noise stopped. Turner looked up and saw Rose Vandel enter. She wore a purple satin dress, cut low on top and short on the bottom. Women frowned at her and men smiled. But the men kept their distance.

Rose Vandel looked around, obviously looking for a place to sit. Turner waved, got her attention and motioned her to his table. When he stood up and held her chair for her, a loud *hurrumph* came from one of the women customers.

'Thank you, Mr. Turner,' she said, 'but aren't you afraid of what people will think of you?'

'After the way you befriended Mrs. Mahoney, I can't let you stand. You're welcome at my table anytime.'

'How is the chopped buckskin?' she asked, nodding toward his plate.

'Good if you can chew bones.'

She threw her head back and laughed a healthy laugh. 'You're not so stuffy after all, Mr. Turner. They tell me you're a school teacher. I always thought school teachers went around correcting everyone's grammar and making sure everyone behaved perfectly.'

'I learned long ago, Miss Vandel, that languages are supposed to work for people. People should not have to work for languages. The whole purpose of any language is to communicate, and some of the best communicators I know break every grammatical rule there is.'

She laughed again, bringing forth another disapproval from the front of the room.

Turner finished his meal just as Rose Vandel received hers. He got a refill of coffee and concentrated on it for a moment. 'I heard, Miss Vandel, that you were in the bank when my brother and Mike Mahoney signed an agreement with the banker.'

'Yes, I saw them there.'

'You didn't, by any chance, see what they signed?'

'No. I couldn't see the paper. I saw Mrs. Goodrow put her seal on a paper and sign it herself. Why? George Kemp told everyone that he bought their claim. A lot of people saw them in the bank negotiating something.'

'Yes, but, doggone it, nobody seems to know what they negotiated but George Kemp himself.'

She stopped chewing her food and asked, 'What else could it be?'

'I don't know. I just don't know.'

'But you think something's fishy, as they used to say in St. Louis.'

'I may be all wet, as they say in Kansas, but it just doesn't smell right, as they say in Kansas City.'

She laughed again, and Turner was surprised at how easy it was to talk to Rose Vandel. In fact, he was talking less formally now than he had since the last time he had visited his folks.

'Or,' Rose Vandel laughed, 'as they say in Cripple Creek, it just don't assay out.'

Turner became serious. 'Do you suspect something too?'

'I always have.' She had turned equally serious.

'What do you suspect?'

'I'm like you, Mr. Turner, I only suspect. I don't know a thing.'

'Why do you suspect something?'

'Mr. Turner, maybe I shouldn't say this. I don't want to tell tales out of school or anything. But your brother, he was a nice man and all, but he, uh, we—'

'You knew him?'

'Yes, I knew him. And he was excited about his find. He had all kinds of plans for mining that claim. He talked about it a lot and he never said anything about selling it.'

'This gets more fishy all the time.'

'You're right. And, as they also say in St. Louis, it just plain stinks.'

'You're from St. Louis?'

'Sure. Can't you tell by my Midwestern twang?'

'What brought you here?'

'Gold, the same thing that brought most everybody else. Only I don't intend to dig for it. I'm getting my share, believe me.'

Turner smiled. 'I'll bet you are, Miss Vandel.'

'And doing a public service too,' she said.

Turner's smile widened. 'I can't argue with that.'

★　　★　　★

Turner had to step back for a workman carrying a long board when he returned again to the recorder's building. He went directly to the window nearest the spot where Mrs. Hankins' desk had sat. The rubble had been swept up but the window was still open. He looked outside at the ground and saw nothing but green grass and rocks.

'What're you lookin' for now?' It was Deputy Sheriff Mitchell.

Startled, Turner jerked his head back inside and turned. 'I, uh, I don't know what I'm looking for, Mr. Mitchell. Broken glass, I guess.'

'Find any?'

'No.'

'I'm not surprised. They mucked the place out pretty good.'

Turner shoved his hands deep into his pockets and studied the floor. 'It puzzles me, Mr. Mitchell, that there is no broken glass outside the window. If the glass was broken out by heat, wouldn't some of it have fallen outside?'

'Hell, I don't know, son. I'm just a dumb country deputy sheriff. I do know heat can break out winders. I seen that before in a house fire.'

'Sure, no doubt about that, but—oh well.'

'Still askin' questions, ain't you, son. If you've got any ideas as to who killed your brother, I wish you'd tell me. I'm in a better position to do somethin' about it than you are.'

'If I find anything definite, I'll be sure to let you know.'

'Yeah, well, right now I want you to come over to the jail. I got some men locked up I want you to look at.'

'Why?'

'I got a suspicion they're the ones that beat hell out of you.'

'You locked them up merely on suspicion?'

'That's the only way to keep law and order.'

Turner recognized them immediately: the broad, thick-necked individual with the plaid shirt, and the short man who had beat him while the third held him. They were behind bars in the two-cell jail behind the deputy sheriff's office, and they glared at Turner, daring him with their eyes to identify them.

'You're sure?' asked the lawman.

'No doubt about it,' Turner said.

106

'All right, I'll hold them for the circuit judge. He'll be here tomorrow. You'll have to testify under oath.'

'What kind of punishment are they likely to get?'

'Who knows. Fist fights are so common around here, nobody pays much attention to 'em. Generally, when somebody gets the worst of it, he just takes his licks and keeps his mouth shut. The judge has enough to do tryin' the shooters and knifers.'

'What else is on his docket tomorrow?'

'A theft of some mining tools and an argument over who owns a certain horse.'

'No shooters and knifers?'

'Not this time. There have been plenty of 'em and there'll be more, but not this time.'

'Then he ought to have the time to devote to this case.'

CHAPTER NINE

Judge Sam Topkah was a slender man, six feet tall, with a handlebar moustache and a prominent Adam's apple. He wore a black suit with a coat that came halfway to his knees and a vest with a gold watch chain

107

draped from the right hand pocket to the left hand pocket. He had taken over the deputy's desk while the deputy stood nearby, thumbs hooked inside his gun belt.

Turner stood before the judge, somewhat nervously.

'Just what is it you wanted to see me about, young man?' the judge asked.

'I, uh, I've got a legal question, your honor.'

'It's not my duty to give out free legal advice. If you've got a legal question you ought to consult a lawyer.'

'I may do that eventually, your honor, but I understand the nearest lawyer is in Colorado City. Or Colorado Springs. And that would take at least two days traveling round trip.'

'Oh well, what is your question?' The judge quickly held up one hand, palm outward. 'I'm not promising to answer it, you understand, but I will listen.'

Turner shifted his weight from his left foot to his right, and said, 'Suppose a man said he bought a certain mining claim, but has no bill of sale or anything to prove it?'

'That's simple enough. He has to have a properly signed and notorized document. Otherwise, he does not legally own it.'

'Suppose he says he had the proper paper drawn up, signed and notorized and handed to the recorder, but the recorder's office was destroyed by fire?'

Judge Topkah thought that over a moment, got up from the desk, walked over to the door, looked out at the partially destroyed recorder's building, then sat down again. 'You're not talking about a hypothetical case, are you, young man?'

'No, sir.'

'Are there any witnesses to the transaction?'

'He has witnesses to the fact that a paper was signed and notorized, but apparently only he knows exactly what was on that paper.'

'What about the seller?'

'The sellers are dead, your honor. They were both murdered right after the transaction.'

The judge pondered that bit of news. 'Oh yes, I know what case you're talking about now. It was two prospectors who allegedly sold their claim to Mr. Kemp of The New Gold District Bank, then were murdered when they went back to the claim to collect their belongings.'

'Yes, sir, that's the case.'

'I see. Uhmm. Mr. Kemp alleges he legally purchased their claim, but since the records were destroyed by fire, he has no proof?'

'That's it exactly, your honor.'

'But he does have witnesses to the fact that a transaction of some kind took place?'

'Yes, sir.'

'Uhmm. Well. That is certainly an interesting question.'

'What is your opinion, your honor?'

'Of course I can't issue a ruling without hearing all sides of the case. I would have to hear testimony from Mr. Kemp and from the witnesses. It would all have to be sworn testimony, and then it would be a tough decision to reach.' The judge was quiet a moment, thinking. 'Yes, sir, I don't believe a precedent has ever been set in a case like this one.' He looked at Turner. 'Do you intend to pursue this, young man?'

'I don't know. A legal battle would take time and cost money. Mr. Kemp has the time and money. I have neither. I have to get back home soon.'

'What do you do?'

'I teach at Garden City, Kansas.'

'That's a very honorable profession. I take it your fall term starts soon.'

'Yes, it does.'

'That's too bad. I'd like to see this case tried. It would, no doubt, be appealed to the Supreme Court and I'd like to see how the justices would rule on it.'

'But suppose, your honor, suppose I could prove fraud?'

'If you could prove fraud on the part of the buyer, then the property would go to the next of kin of the sellers. Do you, uh, suspect fraud?'

'I suspect it, your honor, but I can't prove it. Not yet. But I intend to stay here a few more days and see what I can learn.'

'Watch yourself, young man. The law hasn't acquired a very strong hold on this district yet.'

'How long will you be here, your honor?'

The judge looked at a calendar on the wall. 'Oh, I'll be here three or four days. Looks like a light docket. I believe I'll get in some fishing. This is good trout country.'

Turner was the only witness against the three men accused of assault. The husky one, the one who did the talking at the mine, gave his name as Henry Keiger, and said he had been told by Mr. Kemp to keep everyone away. One reason, he said, is they

111

planned to do some blasting, and Mr. Kemp didn't want anyone injured.

The banker, George Kemp, was sworn by the judge and testified that, yes, he did send the men to the mine to do some digging and blasting and bring out some more ore. He wanted more assaying done, he said, to find out more about what kind of property he had there. He took a gamble when he bought it, he said, because only a pack horse load of ore had been assayed. And yes, he did tell the men to keep trespassers away.

But, he added quickly and loudly, he would have no lawbreakers in his employ, and he recommended that the men be fined.

Judge Topkah said their method of dealing with trespassers was rather harsh, and he found them guilty of assault. He fined them ten dollars each and ordered them released from confinement. The judge admonished Turner for trying to force his way at the mine and advised him to get permission before returning for the tent. Turner said he would do so.

'All right, Mr. Turner,' George Kemp said, 'you can take down that tent and carry it away. But I don't want you prowling around that mine or any of the equipment we have there. It's very easy for a tenderfoot to get hurt, you know.'

The trial was over but they were still inside the sheriff's office-courtroom along with a handful of townspeople who had come to see justice in action. George Kemp raised his voice to make certain he was heard by everyone. 'However, these men have been punished upon my recommendation, and they will bother you no further.'

The burlap bag half full of gold ore was heavy and Turner was short of breath as he lugged it into an assayer's office. He had identified the office by a large handpainted sign over the door.

A medium-sized man with a moustache and a sleepy look on his face took one of the rocks and looked it over, turning it in his hand several times.

'Where'd it come from?' he asked.

Turner told him.

'Oh yes. I assayed some other ore from that hole. It looked good. It was brought in by a Mr. Mike Mahoney.'

'How good?'

'Oh, about two hundred dollars a ton, I'd say.'

'Is that good?'

The assayer put the rock back in the sack and clapped his hands to rid them of any loose dirt. 'Oh yes. Not the best. But good. Very good.'

'Then it had been proven that mine is a valuable one?'

'I'd say so. Yes, I wish I owned it.'

⋆ ⋆ ⋆

The three thugs were near the tent when Turner rode down the hill to it. They said nothing, but the burly one named Keiger grabbed a rifle and kept it in his hands as Turner dismounted and tied his horses to a tree. He was riding the bay mare and leading the gray horse that had belonged to Mike Mahoney. The gray horse would have to carry the tent back to town.

What he would do with it, Turner had not decided. Sell it, if he found a buyer, or give it away. His real purpose for going after it was to get another look at the camp and campsite. What he was looking for, he didn't know. Anything. Any kind of clue.

He walked inside the tent and looked around. Nothing had been moved. He examined the walls again, hoping to find

114

more pencil marks. He found none. He puzzled again over the faint marks he had found earlier. The only marks that didn't make sense were the ones that read: 20,000 × 4.

Were the partners multiplying twenty thousand dollars by four? Were they dividing twenty thousand four ways? Why?

After a while, Turner went out and began pulling up the tent stakes. The three men watched. They had stopped working and were just watching him with hard eyes.

He pulled up ten stakes and got the tent down. He rolled it up and lifted it once to see how heavy it was. He estimated it weighed one hundred and fifty pounds. He untied the gray horse and led him over to the tent. 'Just stand there and don't move,' he said aloud, 'while I wrestle this thing up onto your saddle.'

He got one end up, got his shoulder under it and straightened his legs. That was when he felt the muzzle of the gun pressed against his back.

'Drop it, bloomer button.'

He looked behind him and saw Keiger with the rifle. The other two were standing beside Keiger. The rifle was shoved harder against him.

'Drop it and turn around, or I'll blast your spine in two.'

Turner dropped the tent. The gray horse snorted at the falling object and sidestepped away from it, dragging his halter rope.

'Turn around.'

Turner did as he was told, watchful. 'Listen,' he said, 'your boss told you I was coming for the tent. You've got no right to—'

'Shut up.' Keiger held the rifle with one hand and hit Turner in the face with the other. Turner staggered back two steps. Blood spurted from his nose.

'You had to go to the law, didn't you?' Keiger said. 'Couldn't take a lickin' without goin' to the law. Got us arrested and locked up and fined ten dollars apiece. Well, you owe us thirty dollars.'

Blood was running down Turner's chin and dripping onto his shirt. He was scared, but trying not to show it. 'Listen, in the first place I didn't go to the deputy sheriff. He came to me. I didn't complain until he asked what had happened. And in the second place, I don't have thirty dollars in my pocket. I didn't carry my wallet.'

Keiger grinned cruelly. 'Well, then,

we'll just have to take it out of your hide.'

'If you beat me again, the deputy sheriff will just arrest you again.'

'Beat you?' Keiger chuckled. 'Hell, I ain't gonna touch you again. I'm just gonna put a slug in your gut and watch you die.'

His finger tightened on the trigger. The rifle was pointed right at Turner's stomach. Turner knew that if the thug's finger tightened another fraction of an inch, the gun would fire and a heavy slug would rip into his intestines, causing him death. His stomach muscles tightened in fear and anticipation.

'No, don't. Listen, if you shoot me the deputy sheriff will know who did it. You'll be hung for murder.'

Keiger's cruel grin returned. 'I got a hunch that deputy don't care what happens to you. Say your prayers.'

The short man spoke. 'That deputy probably don't care what happens to 'im, but he's just itchin' to hang them murders on somebody. Make hisself look good.'

The third man added, 'That deputy shoots purty fast. He might shoot us full of holes and blame us for them murders after we're dead.'

Keiger's trigger finger relaxed. He stared

hard at Turner. 'Don't go countin' your blessin's yet. I ain't through with you.'

Turner's breathing came a little easier. The deputy sheriff's quick gun may have saved his life again.

The short man warned the others that if Turner were freed, he would go straight to the deputy and report what had happened. 'We can't let 'im go now. You started something, Keiger, and now we have to finish it.'

'Lemme think a minute,' said Keiger. He backed away from Turner, but held the rifle steady, pointed at him. 'Tie 'im up.'

The short man pulled a skinning knife from a holster on his belt, bent over the tent, and cut a four-foot piece off the tent rope. He grabbed Turner's hands, pulled them back and tied them behind Turner's back. The rope restricted blood circulation and it was painful.

'Now lemme think,' said Keiger. 'We cain't let 'im go back to ol' Mitchell. We'd have to leave the country. Besides, Mr. Kemp said somethin' about how he'd like to see this gent disapear. He might pay us a bonus if ol' bloomer button here ain't never seen again.'

'We'll have to kill 'im and hide his body,'

said the third man.

'Yeah, that's the thing to do,' Keiger replied. 'But where?'

'I know a place.' It was the short man. 'An old drift.'

'Ain't there nobody around there, Shorty?' Keiger asked.

'Nope. They gave up on 'er, but it goes back a couple hunnerd yards. We can dump 'im in there and blast it shut, and he'll be buried forever.'

The thought of being buried alive sent a chill coursing through Turner's body. Fear knotted his stomach muscles again. He tried to speak but no words came out.

Keiger snorted, then chuckled. 'Where is it?'

'Two, two and a half miles from here, across the creek and over the hill.' He pointed north.

Keiger chuckled again. A cruel light came on in his eyes. 'That's what we'll do. Nobody is gonna knock me down, get me thrown in jail and fined ten dollars and live to brag about it.' He raised the rifle and aimed it at Turner's head.

'Wait,' Shorty said. 'We don't wanta carry 'im. Make 'im walk.'

The rifle barrel was lowered. 'Yeah. He's

probably heavy. Git the horses.'

Two men went for the horses while Keiger kept his rifle pointed at Turner. They tightened the cinches, untied Turner's bay mare and led her over.

'I'll hold the reins and you get 'im up on 'er,' Keiger said.

They forced Turner to put his left foot in the stirrup, then pushed and lifted him astraddle the horse. Keiger shoved the rifle into his saddle boot and said, 'Keep your gun on 'im. He might try to jackrabbit.'

'He won't run far,' Shorty said.

Keiger mounted his horse and reached for the bay mare's reins. 'I'll lead this horse. You lead the way.'

Turner felt it was useless, but he tried to reason with the thugs anyway. 'You know you can't get away with this. Deputy Mitchell knows I came over here, and if I don't show up again, he'll know where to look and who to question. Besides, what did I ever do to you gentlemen? As I said, I didn't go to the deputy, he came to me. And as for knocking you down, you hit me first. It was a fair fight. That is, until your pals decided to help out. Then I received plenty of punishment. Why don't we just forget it? Untie me and I'll go get my tent and you'll probably never see me again.'

'Shut up, school teacher,' Keiger said. 'Shut up or I'll knock you off that horse and drag you.'

Turner said no more. He tried his bonds, but he was tied so tightly his hands were numb. He tried to think of a way out of his predicament.

If he had any luck, someone would see the four of them, see that his hands were tied, guess what was happening, and go for help. If he had any luck. At least he was still alive. As long as he was alive there was hope. That's what he tried to convince himself. Why did he do it, he asked himself. He knew these men hated him. When he saw them at the mine he should have left immediately. He guessed, he told himself, he thought they had enough fear of the law that they would mind their own business. The law. Only Deputy Sheriff Mitchell's fast gun kept any semblance of law in that part of the nation. The deputy was a man who shot first and then conducted a trial. The hoodlums feared him and stayed out of his way. Gun law was the only law that had any effect. No wonder Lemual wore his .44 everywhere he went. No wonder everyone carried a gun. It wasn't wild animals they feared. It was men. If he had it to do over again, Turner decided, he would carry Lem's .44.

They rode over a high steep hill and down the other side. They followed a nearly dry creek a short distance, then went up through the timber, over another hill and across another creek hidden by willows.

Turner saw the headframe and the mine dump before he saw the hole in the ground. A skip stood on the ground with the cable still attached and looped over the pulley on the headframe.

'We cain't ride down in that, Shorty,' Keiger said, nodding toward the skip. 'It takes mule power to run that hoist.'

'I wasn't plannin' to go down that shaft,' Shorty replied. He pointed to another steep hill a short distance away. 'There's another shaft over there in the side of that mountain, a hor'zontal shaft. They blasted in a couple hunnerd yards before they gave up. There's still some powder in there.'

Keiger turned his horse toward a hole that could be seen in the side of the far hill and pulled the bay mare along behind him. Another pile of broken rock lay around the mouth of the shaft, and an overturned ore

122

car lay beside two broken rails. The rails led into the mine shaft. The opening was partially supported by eight-inch wide timbers, but one timber was broken and part of the mountain had fallen in front of the opening.

'They spent a lot of money on this one before they gave up,' Shorty said. 'They thought they had a vein but it petered out. They left some powder inside. It's still good.'

'I get you,' said Keiger. 'We knock him in the head, put his carcass in there and blow up the mountain. Nobody'll ever find 'im.'

'Sure. That deputy'll never know what happened to 'im.' Shorty turned to the other man. 'Will he, Pickett?'

Pickett spoke next. 'He'll know somethin' happened to 'im and he'll be asking questions.'

'Not if ol' Kemp tells 'im not to,' Keiger said. 'And I don't think ol' Kemp wants 'im askin' too many questions.'

'He can ask all day,' said Shorty, 'and I'll just claim I never saw this yahoo again. I'd leave the country but we know too much about that banker, and he's gonna keep payin' us better wages.'

'He'll pay,' Pickett put in, 'just like he paid them fines. Besides, he as much as said he'd like to see this gunsel disappear. He didn't say how.'

Keiger chuckled. 'He'll disappear all right.'

'We sure cain't let 'im go now,' Pickett said.

Keiger dismounted. 'Let's get on with it. Where is that powder?'

Shorty entered the shaft and hollered back. 'Here it is, a whole box of it. They had all kinds of powder here to blast a hole in this mountain.'

'Did you find some caps?' Keiger yelled.

'Yeah, a bunch of 'em. Caps, fuses and everything.'

'You set the charge and I'll take care of him.'

Shorty tied eight sticks of dynamite together with a piece of twine, and split one of the sticks with his knife. He placed a blasting cap on the end of a six-foot length of fuse, crimped it onto the fuse with his teeth and inserted it into the split stick.

'Where's the best place to put it?' he yelled.

Pickett pointed to a spot just above the mine entrance. 'Up there. It'll bring the whole mountain down.'

Shorty scrambled up the hill to the spot and looked around. 'We ought to drill in. It'd move a lot more rocks if we could put it back in the ground aways.'

'We ain't got no drill, and I ain't gonna hammer on no damn drill anyway,' Keiger shouted. 'Come on, let's get it done.'

Shorty searched the side of the hill until he found a spot he liked. He shoved one large rock side and scooped out a hole with his hands. 'She's ready,' he shouted. 'Hey, Pickett, bring me a match.'

Keiger pulled his six-gun and cocked the hammer back. 'Git off that horse,' he told Turner.

'Listen,' Turner said, still trying to reason with Keiger. 'I'll just pretend I didn't see you gentlemen today. Just untie me and forget the whole thing.'

'Git down.'

'I can't get down with my hands tied.'

'Fall off then.' Keiger pointed the gun at Turner's head. 'I can kill you now and carry you over there or you can walk over, whatever you want.'

'Listen.' Fear was causing Turner's voice to crack. 'Listen, I mean you no harm. Why are you doing this? Why?'

Pickett was fumbling in his pockets, searching for a match. He stopped and sneered at Turner. 'Listen to 'im beg. Shoot 'im Keiger and let's get back to town. I got a heavy thirst.'

'No, don't,' Turner pleaded. Then the realization hit him. Nothing he could say would change their minds. They were going to kill him. He was tied and helpless and they were going to kill him and bury his body in a mine shaft, and no one would ever know what had happened to him.

He learned something about himself then. He could hate. He hated the men who were doing this to him. And he realized he could not allow his last words to be begging ones.

His voice changed. His lips curled. 'Rot in hell, you yellow sons of bitches.'

Keiger's finger tightened on the trigger. At the same instant, Turner ducked low over the bay mare's neck. The shot spooked the horse and she jumped sideways. Keiger fired again, aiming at Turner's head. The jumping horse spoiled his aim again.

Turner clapped his heels against the mare's sides, and she leaped forward. 'Go Maggie,' he yelled. 'Go like hell.'

The mare stepped on the trailing bridle reins once, but then her speed had the reins flying away from her feet.

Then she accelerated like only an American short horse, forerunner of the quarter horse, could.

More shots were fired, and Keiger swore at his frustration. The horse jumped the brushy cinquefoil, jumped gullys and dodged boulders. Turner was glad he had been a horseman as a youngster and could still sit a saddle. With his hands tied behind him, he leaned over the mare's neck and talked to her. 'Run Maggie. Run like hell, girl.'

She was headed for the willows that grew thick along the creek.

More shots. The mare stumbled and fell.

Turner hit the ground on his left shoulder and scooted on the side of his face. The pain only made him move faster. He glanced back at the horse, saw she was down and not moving, and ran, bending low, for the willows.

He dove into the brush head first, unmindful of being scratched by a hundred willow branches. He fell onto his knees, got up and bored his way through the brush, using his right shoulder as much as he

127

could to shove branches aside. He heard horse's hooves behind him and men cursing. He fell into a shallow gully and lay still, stretched out face up. All he could do was hope he wouldn't be found. Just hope.

Keiger was swearing as loud as he could holler as his horse crashed into the brush. Branches tore at his face and hands, and he had to put his head down and let his broad-brimmed hat protect his face. He swore and spurred his horse deeper into the thicket. The other men followed, hands in front of their faces to ward off the willow whips.

A horse barely missed stepping on Turner's feet, but the rider was protecting his face and didn't see the man stretched out on the ground. Other horses passed nearby and still Turner was not discovered.

Horses were charging through the brush all around him. Men were swearing. Turner lay very still.

'He's in here somewhere,' Keiger yelled. 'We'll find 'im.'

'We got to find 'im.' It was Shorty's voice.

Riders spurred their horses through acres of willows, keeping their faces turned down, trying to push the branches aside with their hands. 'This stuff is so thick a rabbit couldn't get through it,' Shorty yelled. 'There's a million places to hide.'

Keiger pulled up his horse. 'Let's stop and think about it. Come here, will you?'

The three riders gathered in a small clearing. Keiger's shirt was torn, and Shorty had a scratch on his face. 'Let's just think about it,' Keiger said. 'He cain't go far with his hands tied. Let's see now. He came in here right where that dyin' horse is. And he's still in here. There's no place to hide out there.'

'A man on foot can get through this stuff quicker'n a man on a horse,' Shorty said. 'Maybe we ought to hunt on foot.'

'I hate walkin',' said Keiger, 'but we got to find 'im.' He dismounted and the others did the same. 'Let's tie these horses here and split up. Whoever finds 'im, shoot 'im. Don't say nothing, just put a bullet in his gut and let him die lookin' at the hole.'

'Let's go,' said Shorty.

'Wait,' said Pickett. 'What if he gets his hands untied someway. I don't know how, but what if he did? He could sneak over here and get our horses. One of us has gotta stay here.'

'All right,' Keiger said. 'You stay here. Keep the hammer back on that six-shooter

129

and keep your eyes peeled. If you shoot 'im we'll hear it and we'll come back and go on back to town.'

'Which way do you think he went?'

'Probably toward town. He's a town dude.'

'Yeah, he probly cain't wait to tell that deputy sheriff on us.'

Turner heard it all. He knew he had to move. On foot, they would see him. 'Toward town,' they said. He would go the other direction and, hopefully, fool them, Turner decided. He got to his feet, and keeping low, walked stealthily through the brush.

He heard them tramping around several times and each time he lay face down, hoping he would not be discovered. He worked his back toward the abandoned mine. At one point, he looked out into the open and saw the bay mare stretched out on the ground. He realized something else about himself then. He could swear. They shot her. They fatally wounded old Maggie. She would die. The sons of bitches. Kill. That's all they wanted to do. They had killed the horse and they were trying to kill Turner. If by some miracle he got a chance, he would kill those sons of bitches, he vowed.

What? Kill? Yes. His goal was to be a doctor and save lives, but, he swore, *if* I survive this I'll kill those sons of bitches.

Turner heard footsteps coming toward him. He lay down quietly in the thickest clump of bushes he could find. He heard Keiger breathing heavily from the exertion, and swearing steadily. Turner kept his head down and did not look up. More footsteps and Shorty caught up with Keiger.

'Thought you said he'd be goin' toward town?'

'He's tricky,' Keiger said between panting breaths. 'He could be tryin' to fool us.'

'He could be anywhere. There must be twenty acres of these bushes.'

'I'll get 'im if I have to tromp over every damn inch of 'em.'

They moved on, Keiger swearing with every step.

Turner saw a low spot not far away, and he walked on his knees to it. He lay face down in it and discovered he was in black mud. He was there an hour before he heard footsteps again. Whoever was walking nearby was walking in mud. And swearing.

It was Keiger. He stopped. 'Shorty,' he yelled.

An answer came from a hundred yards away.

'Let's git back to the horses. We'll ride over every inch of this stuff. I'm tard of walkin'.'

Shorty agreed. They had to yell at Pickett and get an answer back before they knew in which direction to go to find their horses.

Turner got up and headed again toward the mine. If he could get enough distance between him and the thugs, he had a chance, he told himself. In fact, if he could get to a place across from the mine, he might be wise to leave the willows and hide behind a mine dump, or a boulder, and hope they would continue searching the willows.

Hands tied behind him, Turner bored on, taking more scratches on the face. The left side of his face was already badly skinned from the fall off the horse. His left shoulder was numb from the fall. Slowly, quietly, he went on.

He worked his way to the edge of the willows and found he was near the mine and a mine dump. Still, it was a good seventy-five feet to the nearest cover, a large boulder. Dare he run for it? If he did and a rider happened to be in the open on that side of the creek, he would be seen. And killed.

Turner listened. Silence. He walked on his knees a short distance out of the willows and looked. He saw nothing. Bending low, he scurried for the boulder, half expecting to hear a shout and a shot.

He made it to the boulder and crouched behind it, breathing hard. He stayed there until his breathing returned to normal and he could listen intently. Still, he heard nothing. He mentally measured the distance to a pile of low-grade ore that had been dumped out of the mine. Better cover there, he thought. If I can make it. Listening intently and almost afraid to blink for fear he would miss something, Turner peered from behind the boulder.

The riders were not in sight.

Still running low, he made it to the pile of fractured rock and hit the ground flat. He stayed there several minutes, listening. Perhaps, he would be safer inside the mine. They weren't likely to go in there. It was dark in there, and if they looked in they probably wouldn't see him. Yeah, that was the safest place to hide.

After peering around again, Turner again made a run for cover and ducked inside the horizontal shaft without creating any excitement. He walked carefully, now and then stumbling over rocks in the dark, until he collided with the end of the tunnel. He sat on his heels and hoped.

If he was lucky, the thugs would search every inch of the willows for him and that would take until dark. After dark he would not be so easy to see. After dark perhaps he could walk back to Cripple Creek. It would be a long walk, and by then his hands would probably be ruined from the lack of blood circulation. He had lost all feeling in them long ago.

Wish I could get this rope off, he thought. I've got to get it off. He wondered if by any chance some tools had been left in the shaft. Not likely. But he decided to search the ground behind him with his tied hands anyway.

He concentrated on moving his fingers, and finally got one finger to move, then another. Each movement was painful. Eventually, he could move all his fingers. He began groping the ground behind him, and once he skinned the back of his hand on the edge of a rock.

All he found was rock shattered by dynamite blasts. No tools. His hands came into contact with the sharp rock again. And an idea came to him.

If that rock was sharp enough to skin his hand, maybe it would cut a rope. That is, if he sawed on it long enough.

He groped for the sharp rock again and found it. Working with fingers still partially numb, he placed the rock with the sharp edge up and placed his wrists on either side of it with the rope on top of it. He began a sawing motion. The rock fell over. He righted it and began sawing again. The rock fell over.

It was obvious he could saw on the rope only two or three seconds before the rock fell over. Perhaps he could place it next to another rock or between two rocks. He scooted on the seat of his pants, groping behind him until he found two rocks about the right size. Then he had to find the rock with the sharp edge again. For awhile he was afraid he would never find it again, but finally his fingers came into contact with it. He placed its sharp edge up and carefully, painfully, placed the other rocks on each side of it.

Then he resumed sawing on the rope. The rock fell over.

Patiently, he got the three rocks in place and continued sawing. He got in about twenty seconds of sawing before the rock fell over again. He righted it and sawed.

One strand in the rope parted.

With renewed hope, he sawed. Soon another strand parted. How many strands in the rope? he wondered. Probably three. Most grass ropes have three strands. He sawed. The rock fell over. He righted it and sawed.

Suddenly his hands were free.

And suddenly the blood returned to his hands, painfully. It felt as if a thousand needles were being forced into his flesh. He wrung his hands. A small moan escaped him. His wrists were raw. But slowly the pain subsided.

CHAPTER TEN

Steel shod hooves striking rocks reminded him of his first problem. He looked up at the tunnel entrance and saw a horse's legs. Keiger was still swearing. 'Where in the humped-up hell can that yahoo be? I know damn well he didn't get out of this valley.'

'Aw, he's probly tunneled back in those willer bushes where nobody can find 'im.' It was Shorty's voice.

'You don't think that lucky white-collared yahoo could have crawled on his belly and got over the hill?'

'If he did he's got a mighty sore belly by now. Naw, he's around here. We better ride those bushes some more. Maybe one of these horses'll step on 'im.'

'We gotta find 'im in a hour or hour and a half. It's gonna get dark.'

'Tell you what, Keiger. If we don't find 'im, I'm gonna hunt up that banker, draw my money and hightail it. I don't want that deputy sheriff after me.'

'What if the old thief won't pay us?'

'He'll have to. We know too much about 'im. And he hinted he'd pay us a bonus if that Turner was to disappear.'

Human legs appeared in the tunnel entrance, and Keiger's face appeared. He was squatting beside his horse, peering inside. He apparently saw nothing. It was pitch dark inside and Turner had flattened out behind some of the broken rock. Then they were gone, their voices fading away.

What did Keiger say? The banker wanted him to disappear? It was the second time one of the three had said that. Why? Was George Kemp putting on an act when he recommended that they be fined? Was he trying to make the townspeople think he would have nothing to do with lawlessness? Turner vowed he would find answers to those questions. And some others.

He felt safer now that the riders had left the mine entrance without coming inside. He hoped for darkness soon so he could make his way back to Cripple Creek.

He took stock of his situation. His left shoulder was beginning to ache. His face was skinned up and scratched. His shirt was torn and bloody. And his wrists were raw and bleeding. Otherwise he was in good shape. Able to walk, anyhow, he told himself.

He sat with his back against the tunnel wall and watched daylight slowly fade from the entrance. Eventually, it was dark. Slowly, he groped, stumbled and staggered to the entrance and looked out. Only a sliver of daylight was left on the western horizon. He neither saw nor heard any other signs of life.

Time to go.

Let's see. Across the creek and over a hill in front of him, across a valley and over another hill and he'd come to Lem's camp. Follow the creek or go over another hill to the Canon City road. Then back to Cripple Creek. He wondered if his tired legs could carry him. Only one way to find out. Put one foot in front of the other.

The quarter moon put out so little light that Turner couldn't even see the horizon, but he started out strong, happy just to be alive. If the thugs were still around, he would probably hear them in time to hide in the darkness. Yes, he was safe now. But it was a long way to Cripple Creek.

Bill Turner knew the mine entrance faced the direction he had to go, and he picked out a star brighter than the rest to guide him. He wished he had studied astronomy at the university. It would have helped him find his directions. But he hoped that bright star would stay where it was, and whatever it was, it would guide him. The night air turned chilly, then cold. Turner stumbled along, stubbing his toes over the rocks and tree roots. He groped his way through the willows and across the creek, falling twice. Instead of cursing the bushes, he silently thanked them. They had saved his life.

He topped the first hill and saw nothing but night blackness ahead. The night cold was getting to him. He walked faster and tried to keep his teeth from chattering.

His left shoulder was aching steadily now, and the side of his face burned. He walked on, across a narrow valley and up another hill.

'Put one foot in front of the other,' he said aloud. 'Keep going.'

He caught himself staggering with fatigue. His legs felt weak. He tried talking to himself to stay awake. Wonder if anyone misses me? Is the deputy sheriff looking for me? Naw. Not yet. How about Mrs. Mahoney? Is she worried? She must have known by now that something has happened. Has she reported it to Deputy Mitchell? She's quite a woman. Quiet, dignified, proud. But decisive when she needs to be. Capable. Stronger than she looks. Obviously a lady brought up in a well-to-do family, but not so far above the crowd that she can't be sociable with a prostitute who befriended her when she had no other friends. She must have a spark of adventure in her. Otherwise she would not have married a man like Mike

Mahoney. Yes, she's quite a woman. Pretty too.

A doctor's daughter. She would make a good doctor's wife. What are you saying, Bill Turner? You're not a doctor, and unless you find a gold mine yourself, you never will be. Besides, she's got too much on her mind to pay attention to another man. At least for a long time. Forget it, Bill Turner. First things first.

'First I have to survive,' he said aloud.

Keeping an eye on the star, Turner stumbled and staggered on. He topped another hill and started downhill. Lem's camp had to be at the bottom of this hill, he thought. No, it was across a creek from this hill. A creek. There's water in the creek. He was reminded that he had had no water since early the day before, and his lips and throat were dry. That water was going to taste very good. He stumbled on. The quarter moon was still sitting on the horizon to his left. Must be east. Yes, that would make sense. If that's east then I'm going in the right direction. The moon was providing a little more light now, but not much more than it did when Turner started his walk. Turner staggered on.

A dark mass loomed before him. Like a

long, low building. Can't be. He reached out to touch it and found it was farther away than he had thought. He kept walking. The mass was right in front of him then and he discovered it was a clump of willows. The creek. He was at the creek.

Parting the branches with his hands, Turner made his way forward, carefully. He stumbled and fell onto his hands and knees into the creek. The water was cold and it felt and tasted good. Turner put his face in it and sipped water through dry lips. It was a lifesaver. A man can go a long time without food, but not so long without water, he knew. Not even in a cold climate.

He stayed there until the coldness made his hands and knees numb, then he stood up, climbed the low creek bank and began groping his way through the brush. He collected another scratch or two before he found his way out.

'Now where am I?' he said aloud. If his calculations were correct, Lem's camp would be directly ahead of him. He wished that the sliver of a moon would climb a little higher. He walked in the direction of where he hoped the camp would be, then suddenly stopped. What if he fell in the mine in the dark? The fall would break every bone in his body. He would definitely die then. Maybe it would be smart to forget the camp and just follow the creek to the Canon City road. The willows along the creek could barely be seen, but at least they could be seen. He could follow them. He turned toward Cripple Creek and walked, occasionally stumbling over a rock or a clump of grass, trying to keep parallel with the line of willows.

He stumbled over something soft, something about knee-high. He squatted and felt of it with his hands. It was the rolled up tent. He had found Lem's camp and the tent and he had not fallen into the mine.

With trembling fingers, he unrolled a portion of the tent. It was soft and warm, and he was very cold and tired. He lay down and pulled a corner of the canvas over him.

He slept.

It was hoofbeats that awakened him. Hearing them, he came awake suddenly, instantly alert. He sat up and glanced up the creek. Nothing there. He looked up the hill toward the Canon City road and still saw nothing. The hoofbeats came from behind him, and he turned, climbing to his feet at the same time. He saw what it was then.

It was the gray gelding, the one that had belonged to Mike Mahoney. The horse was still saddled and grazing not far from where he had been left when the three thugs had ridden away with Turner as their captive.

Turner's left shoulder was aching fiercely now. He walked toward the horse. The horse raised its head and watched him approach. It sidestepped away from the trailing halter rope, then stopped and waited. Turner picked up the rope first, then touched the horse on the neck. 'Good boy. Boy, do I need you.'

He realized he had no bridle and would have to handle the horse with nothing on its head but the halter. Only the gentlest of horses could be handled that way. He gathered the six-foot halter rope and got hold of the saddle horn. He pulled himself stiffly into the saddle as the gray gelding waited patiently. 'Someone trained you well,' Turner said to the horse. 'All right, take your time but carry me back to town, will you?'

The horse stepped right out, turned the way Turner pulled its head, and seemed glad to be going somewhere.

Horse and rider approached the town from the south and drew only a few stares from men on the streets as they made their way to the stables.

The stableman's jaw sprung open again, and a tiny stream of tobacco juice ran down the corner of his mouth. 'Good gawd, have you done gone and got yourself hurt again?'

Turner managed a wry grin. 'Not too badly. The horse fell with me.'

'Danged if you ain't one for gettin' hurt. Fall off a horse and now a horse turns over with you. You better take care of that.' He pointed to Turner's skinned face.

Turner allowed he would. He unsaddled the horse with one hand and handed the lead rope to the stableman. He got the man's promise that the animal would be well fed, then walked on sore feet to the Bluebird Hotel.

Again he walked through the lobby and up the stairs without saying a word to anyone, hoping no one would notice the condition he was in.

Inside his room, he poured water into the washbasin and gingerly washed his face. He couldn't help glancing at the bed but he was determined he was going to stay off it. If he even so much as sat on it, he would be sound asleep in minutes, he knew. He couldn't do that. He had other things to do.

He opened his valise and took out his shaving kit, then changed his mind. Let the beard grow. Worse things could happen.

Again there came a soft knock on the door, and again Mrs. Mahoney stood there. 'You're hurt again, aren't you?' she said. 'I was in the dining room when you walked through the lobby. I've been worried. What happened?'

'I, uh, had an accident. A horse fell with me.'

She stepped close and touched the side of his face with soft fingers. 'That's a bad bruise. You can't ignore wounds like that.'

Turner grinned crookedly. 'It's a long way from any vital organs. I'll live.'

She smiled, showing even white teeth. It occurred to Turner that he had not seen her smile before.

'You're a big tough he-man, aren't you? It would never do to admit you're injured.'

Turner's smile spread, but pain forced his features straight again. 'Well, uh, to tell the truth, my left shoulder hurts more than anything else. Do you know how to bind a shoulder?'

'Let me see it.' She began unbuttoning

146

Turner's shirt. He grabbed her hands. It was modesty.

'No, let me do it.' Working with one hand, he got his shirt off, walked over to a mirror and examined himself. 'Can't tell if anything is broken. Might just be bruised.'

'Yes, and it just might be fractured,' she said sternly. 'You ought to see a doctor as soon as possible.'

'No, not now. Tomorrow maybe I'll travel to Colorado Springs. But not now.'

'Why? What's so urgent?'

He turned to face her. 'Listen, Mrs. Mahoney. There have been some crooked dealings over that mine. Your husband's and my brother's. That banker didn't buy that mine. Oh, he had some dealings with them, I don't know what. Perhaps they merely borrowed money from him to build a road and start mining. I don't know. But I'm almost convinced that banker didn't buy that mine.'

Her eyes widened. 'You are convinced, aren't you? Can you prove it? Can I help?'

'No, I can't prove it yet, but I'm going to. Some way. There's got to be some way. Listen, there are three hoodlums here in town who are on that banker's payroll, and they might know what happened. I've got

147

to find them.'

She gave him an accusing look. 'They are the three men who beat you up, aren't they? And they are extremely dangerous. Are they, by any chance, responsible for what happened to you last night?'

He didn't answer, but instead started trying to wrap his shoulder in a towel.

'Here, let me help.' She wrapped the towel expertly around his shoulder and left upper arm. 'I need something to pin it with. I've got some pins in my room. I'll be right back.'

When she left, Turner opened his brother's satchel and took out the .44. With one hand, he managed to fasten the belt around his waist and holster the gun. The gun was fully loaded and there were more cartridges in the belt loops. Then Mrs. Mahoney was back.

She stopped suddenly when she saw the gun, but she said nothing about it. She had brought pins and more cloth, and she stepped up to him and bound his shoulder tightly, then made a sling for his arm.

'Keep your arm still and hopefully you won't aggravate the injury,' she said. 'I do wish you would forget that mine for a while and go find a doctor.'

'I can't forget it, Mrs. Mahoney. That's our mine. Yours and mine. Your husband and my brother would want us to have it. It does not belong to that crooked banker.'

The worry creases between her eyes deepened. 'It's not worth your getting killed. Nothing is worth that. There has been enough killing over that mine.'

She gingerly touched the butt of the gun he was wearing. 'And I know there will be more men killed.' Suddenly she broke into tears. 'I don't want you to lose your life too, Mr. Turner. Please don't. Please, just get on the stage and leave, will you?'

Her tears almost convinced Turner that she was right. No woman, except his mother, had ever showed that much concern for him. But he knew he could not leave. Not yet. 'I don't intend to be another victim, Mrs. Mahoney. I'll be careful. I promise.'

She wiped her eyes with a dainty handkerchief that she took out of her dress pocket. 'I'm sorry. I have no right to ask anything of you. It's just that you're a fine and decent man and I don't want anything to happen to you.'

Turner stepped away from her. He struggled to put his shirt on with one hand.

She helped him. He turned his back as he tucked the tail into his pants. When he turned around again, she had started for the door.

'Will you wait one more day, Mrs. Mahoney? I, uh, I'd like you to.'

'Yes,' she said quietly. 'I'll stay another day. Please be careful.' With that, she left the room.

CHAPTER ELEVEN

'Now don't tell me you fell off a horse again,' Deputy Sheriff Mitchell squinted at Turner.

'No, this time the horse fell.' It wasn't a lie but it wasn't the whole truth either.

'You sure got a talent for gettin' skinned up.' The deputy was behind his desk, his booted and spurred feet on the upside-down wastebasket again. His hat was shoved back and he was rolling a cigarette.

'Mr. Mitchell, do you happen to know where I could find those men, the ones you arrested for assault?'

'I ain't seen 'em since yestiddy mornin', but my part-time deputy said he seen 'em early this mornin'. Said they was waitin' for the bank to open. Why? They do that to you? And what're you packin' that iron for? You lookin' for trouble?'

Turner ignored the question. He turned and walked out and up the street to the bank. The lobby was nearly deserted, and people at desks and behind tellers' cages stared at Turner. George Kemp looked up at the shadow in his office door. His eyes widened in surprise, his mouth opened and he stammered, 'You, uh, you. Where, uh what?'

'Yes, it's me, Mr. Kemp. Thought you'd never see me alive again, didn't you? Your hired hoodlums fell down on the job.'

The banker quickly regained his composure. 'What are you talking about? What hired hoodlums?'

'You know very well. The ones who asaulted me two days ago. They did it again, only this time they intended to kill me. They work for you and I have to assume they were carrying out your orders.'

'Say you can't—you can't come in here making accusations like that. We have some law in this town. I'll have you arrested.'

Turner ignored the threat. 'Where are they?'

'I have no idea and I wouldn't tell you if I did.'

Turner started to leave, then stopped and looked back. 'I'll be seeing you again, Mr. Kemp. We've got plenty to talk about.'

He searched the two cafes and the three bars in town and didn't find them. The hotel clerk said nobody fitting that description was registered there. The stableman said he hadn't seen them since the day before yesterday. They had to have left town. But which way did they go? It was either to Florissant or out on the east road, or over the road to Canon City.

Turner hated to pull the gray gelding away from the feed rack, but he needed the horse. He managed to throw the saddle on him and cinch it up with one hand. Awkwardly, he climbed into the saddle and headed the gelding down Bennett Avenue toward Florissant. At the edge of town he asked a man working in a mine dump if he had seen the three. No, he was told.

The gelding carried him back to the east road, where he met a rancher coming toward him in a light wagon. He asked the same question and got the same answer.

They had to be heading for Canon City. Turner knew they were getting farther away from him all the time but he had to know which way they were going before he went in pursuit.

With spurless shoes in the stirrups, Turner prodded the gray gelding into a slow gallop down the Canon City road. It was luck, he knew, that the three hoodlums had had to wait for the bank to open to get their pay from George Kemp. Otherwise, he would have met them on his way to town, while he was unarmed. Now, instead of the three looking for him, he was looking for them.

But what would he do if he caught them? It would be three to one, and they were well armed.

'First things first,' he said to the horse. 'We've got to catch them first.'

Soon he knew he was on their trail. He met three freight wagons pulled by four-horse teams, hauling supplies and tools to the mining town of Cripple Creek. When they pulled abreast, Turner reined his horse alongside the lead wagon long enough to get information out of the driver. Yes, three men on horseback leading a pack horse had passed them an hour earlier. They had been riding at a slow trot, but their horses seemed tired and looked as if they needed feed and rest.

The teamster stared at Turner's skinned face and bandaged shoulder but politely refrained from asking about it. Turner could overtake the three if his own horse didn't give out, the teamster said.

Turner voiced his thanks and urged the gray into a slow gallop again. It would be typical of the three bullies to leave their horses tied while they waited for the bank to open. The men were miners, not horsemen, and like most nonhorsemen they didn't seem to understand that horses are flesh and blood. They have to eat, drink and rest like any other animal, human or otherwise. Not only that, when horses get tired, it takes them a long time to recuperate. And when horses are hungry, it takes them hours to eat their fill. Turner had grown up with horses and he knew all that.

The gray had had a saddle on him all day and all night, but he was rested and fed and still loping along easily. Turner felt the breeze ruffle his hair and realized again how pleasant it was to be riding in the mountains. Yes, it was pleasant.

But he had a very unpleasant and dangerous job to do.

The road was narrow, rocky and steep in places. In places, the terrain on one side of the road went almost straight up and on the other it dropped into a creek. The road passed several small grassy parks where deer grazed alongside cattle. Turner saw more deer than cattle.

He kept his vision aimed as far ahead as the landscape would allow, and before he rounded each of the many curves, he slowed the horse to a walk and made certain the road ahead was clear.

The gray galloped on. Turner was tiring much faster than the horse. He was reminded that he had had very little rest after a terrifying ordeal the night before, and only a light breakfast. His left shoulder ached, and he feared he had suffered a fracture. How long could he ignore it before real trouble set in? he asked himself. That's just one of the things he would have learned in medical school. But perhaps it wasn't broken, just dislocated or badly bruised. He didn't know. In that case, it would be painful, but no permanent damage would have been done.

He came to a sharp curve and pulled the gray to a stop. He walked the horse forward cautiously until he could see that the road ahead was clear. On they went, the gray sweating and puffing now. He slowed the horse to a trot, but the rough gait hurt his shoulder with every step. They traveled at a walk for a time, until the horse got its wind, then Turner urged it again into a slow gallop.

Four miles farther along they came to another curve. Turner lifted his reins and brought the horse to a stop. He approached the bend cautiously. He saw them.

They were riding at a trot. One horse and rider was lagging behind and the rider was whipping and cursing the horse. Keiger.

Turner could hear him swearing from two hundred yards away. The bullnecked man with the jackboots was using a length of rope to whip his horse on. The horse looked to be past caring what happened. And Shorty, the mean little man, was yelling something back at Keiger. Only Pickett, the third partner, was riding on.

Turner quit the road and rode up a steep hill, so steep the gray gelding had to scramble to get to the top. There he was in a thick grove of young aspens and he could see the men without being seen.

Keiger suddenly dismounted and pulled the saddle, rifle boot and all, off his horse. Then he grabbed the lead rope on the pack horse and untied the pack. He jerked bedrolls, skillets and canned food off the pack horse and started to mount. But on second thought, he pulled his six-gun and shot the heaving saddle horse squarely between the eyes. The shot echoed among the hills for several seconds. The horse dropped immediately.

'Why you mean son of a bitch,' Turner muttered. 'Ride a horse half to death then kill it because it can't go any farther. You mean son of a bitch.'

He had an urge to gallop down there, shooting. See how many of them he could knock out of their saddles before they knew what was happening. Keiger would be his first target. He'd get Keiger even if he got no one else. 'I'll get you, you son of a bitch,' Turner muttered.

But the pack horse was probably fresh that morning. Keiger was now mounted again, and he was leading the way at a fast trot.

Turner knew he could never get ahead of them that day. And what if he did? The best he could hope to do was surprise them as they rounded a curve in the road and get the drop on them. That would be extremely dangerous, he knew, because there were three of them and they knew how to handle guns.

I should have brought the deputy sheriff, Turner thought. He would know what to do. His fast gun would have all three of them in the dirt before they knew what happened. The way he did it in the Spotted Pup Saloon. Before Turner had even known of the danger, the deputy's gun had barked three times in rapid succession and three men had died. Deputy Sheriff Mitchell is a killer, but his kind is what it takes to civilize the West, Turner thought.

Civilization is great, but it has to be earned. And owing to human nature, men have to die for it. The frontier West was not yet civilized.

The trick, Turner said to himself, is to make the guilty men die, not the innocent ones.

He sat his horse on top of the hill and watched the three hoodlums ride out of sight. The thing to do, he decided, was to keep them in sight until dark when they made camp, then attack in the dark.

He rode off the hill and followed his quarry, keeping his distance and approaching the curves with a great deal of care.

Dark was slow coming. The sun seemed to set on top of the range of mountains to the west and camp there. The gray gelding was tiring, and Turner was having a hard time keeping awake in the saddle. Once he rode around a curve carelessly and saw the men not more than a hundred yards ahead. He stopped his horse immediately, and hoped he had not been seen. The three hoodlums rode on, Keiger in the lead.

Finally, the sun slipped down behind the mountains. Its rays reflected upward onto a bank of clouds, turning them bright red. Darkness would come soon. Turner slowed the gray to a walk, biding his time now.

Ahead a short distance, the road paralleled a creek and followed it a half dozen miles. It wasn't quite dark when he saw the campfire near the creek.

CHAPTER TWELVE

Turner stopped immediately and reined his horse off the opposite side of the road. Again, the country was steep there, and the horse had to scramble. Once in the thick timber at the top of a ridge, he dismounted and watched the fire. He could see figures moving around it, but only two. Where was the third? He decided to get closer, then make plans.

At first he walked and led the gray gelding, then he remembered that horses could see quite well in the dark and he knew it would be safer to ride. He rode uphill, downhill and through ponderosas and lodge pole pines. He was made to understand why cowboys wore broadbrimmed hats. The brims helped protect riders' faces as they rode in the timber and brush. Turner had no such protection, and his sore face collected more scratches.

The horse stopped suddenly, and Turner guessed there was a sharp drop somewhere ahead, something the horse could sense but he could not. Remembering the night before, Turner wondered if he was destined to spend the rest of his life groping in the dark. He realized it was a good thing the horse could see because he couldn't. He turned the horse downhill and the animal went readily. Soon they came out of the timber and Turner saw they were only about five hundred yards away from the campfire. They were still uphill from it and Turner could look right down at Shorty and Pickett. Where was Keiger?

Keiger, Turner decided, was probably standing guard, still afraid the deputy sheriff might be coming for them. He was, no doubt, looking down the road where they came from. Hopefully, they weren't expecting an attack from up there.

Attack? How? If he had a rifle and a little moonlight he could pick off the two of them. But could he shoot down unsuspecting men? Could he just ambush them? That's the way his brother and Mike Mahoney had died. At least that's what the deputy sheriff had said. But Turner knew he could not kill that way. In fact, now that the time had come, he wasn't sure he could kill at all. Anyway, he silently told himself, I'm not going to go down there and challenge them to a duel.

He tied the horse to a small aspen and started walking and sliding downhill. He looked back and wondered if he would be able to find the horse again in the dark. He could not ride the horse any closer, he knew. It might sense the other horse and nicker at them, putting the thugs on the alert. He tried to pick out a landmark, but he could see only a few feet ahead.

Thinking of the horses gave him an idea. The horses were no doubt tied nearby, and if the men had any sense they would be picketed so they could graze. That means they would be out of sight of the camp. Find them and cut them loose, that's the thing to do, he thought. Put those thugs afoot. That would be doing the horses a favor too.

He knew he had reached the road when the ground leveled out. The fire was still downhill a ways, but within easy hollering distance now. Keiger was no doubt somewhere nearby. Walking silently, Turner crossed the road and stopped behind a huge boulder. He could hear the men talking and cursing.

'That goddam Keiger had to kill his horse and leave our bedrolls and chuck back there on the road,' Shorty was saying.

'If I ever get to Canon City, I'm going to cut and run from that son of a bitch,' Pickett said. 'He's crazy enough to get us all killed.'

Shorty got up and put another piece of wood on the fire. 'Jaysus, it's cold in these mountains.'

Pickett stood up, hugged himself, shivered, and said he was going to see how the horses were doing. 'That fool horse of mine'll probably kill hisself gettin' tangled up in the rope,' he said.

He left the small circle of light created by the fire, and Turner watched him go, trying to follow him with his eyes in the darkness to see where the horses were.

Never look directly at the object you want to see in the dark. That was something he had read somewhere. Look to the side of it. He tried it. Soon a dark shape became discernible. It was a horse only about thirty feet from the fire. That's one. The others can't be far away, although they would have to be at least a picket rope's length from each other. If not, they would get their ropes tangled.

Turner guessed that the horses were all staked out in the tall swamp grass that seemed to grow along all the creeks. That would be the most sensible place for them. He waited until Pickett returned to the fire and sat on the ground, hugging his knees. Then he walked cautiously toward the horse he had spotted.

He tripped over the stake rope before he found the horse. Groping with his hands, he identified the rope for what it was and followed it to the horse. The horse was gentle and didn't try to pull away. Slipping the halter off was a simple task. The horse was free, but it did not realize it or did not care. It kept on cropping the grass.

Keeping his feet close to the ground, Turner walked with shuffling steps in search of the other horses. Soon he discovered another rope and followed it to a horse. The halter had a knot in it and it took a while for Turner to get it untied in the dark, but soon that horse too was free.

Standing still and listening, Turner heard the third animal's hoof strike the ground to his left, farther away from the fire. His eyes separated the dark shape from other night shapes, and he unbuckled the halter on that horse.

The horses were so hungry they continued feeding, but Turner knew they would eventually wander away. The three thugs would be afoot.

Now what? So they were afoot, a fate considered by many Westerners to be horrible. But that was not always so. The Canon City road was traveled every day and the hoodlums would get a ride on a freight wagon sooner or later.

The punishment had to be more severe.

Turner remembered how he felt back at the abandoned mine when they had shot his bay mare. Old Maggie deserved a better fate than that. He had silently vowed to kill them. Hadn't he? Now was his chance.

It would be easy. Creep up to a spot just outside the circle of light and start shooting. He could pick them off before they knew what was happening. Turner hefted the .44. He couldn't miss. That would be the smart thing to do. Don't do anything stupid like asking them to surrender and give them a chance to shoot. They had put Turner through hell, intending to put him to death, and they deserved to die. That's what he had trailed them for, wasn't it? If all he had wanted was to bring them to justice, he should have sent the deputy sheriff.

All right. He made up his mind. Let's get it over with. He walked toward the fire.

He tried to walk silently, but he stumbled over a root and fell noisily onto his knees. He got up quickly, keeping the two men in sight. They didn't move.

Couldn't they hear him coming? Turner stopped and got behind a tree. They didn't seem to be aware of his presence. They must have thought the noise they heard was made by one of the horses. Turner raised the gun and sighted along the barrel, the front sight covering the second button on Shorty's shirt.

He couldn't do it. He could not shoot down an unsuspecting man. He lowered the gun to his side and stood there a moment. Then, without thinking, even before he knew what he was doing, he stepped into the circle of light.

'Good evening, gentlemen,' he said.

Shorty's right hand darted to the six-shooter on his hip. Pickett reached for a rifle leaning against a tree.

'Hold it,' Turner yelled.

Shorty had the gun in his hand, the barrel was coming up, aiming at Turner.

Turner had never in his life pointed a gun at a human being. But now he was facing instant death. It was shoot or be shot. He squeezed the trigger.

The old .44 roared like a canon and the recoil slammed the butt back against Turner's palm. Shorty jerked as if he had been hit in the chest with a brick. He fell backward and lay still. But then Pickett had the rifle in his hands and was swinging the barrel around toward Turner.

Because of his bandaged shoulder, Turner had to cock the .44 with his right hand, his shooting hand, and he was too slow. The rifle barked and a slug tugged at the left side of Turner's shirt. Pickett had been in too much of a hurry to take aim, but he was jacking another cartridge into the firing chamber and he wouldn't miss the second time.

Turner got the hammer back and the .44 roared again. Pickett fell onto his side and rolled onto his back. He tried to get up but fell onto his back again. Then he too was still.

The sound of gunshots bounced around among the mountain peaks for several seconds, then died. For a moment, Turner stood still, somewhat dumbfounded. He had just killed two men. They were dead. A moment ago they were alive and now they were dead. He had killed them.

'My God,' he said aloud. He looked

down at the gun in his hand and the realization came to him that it was a terrible weapon. Just two twitches of his finger and two men were dead. 'My God,' he said again.

It occurred to him that perhaps they were still alive and with the proper medical help could be saved. He had been thinking for years in terms of medicine and medical help. He took a step toward Pickett.

Then a faint sound coming from the direction of the road reminded him that Keiger was out there and he was standing in the fire light, a perfect target.

He turned to scramble into the darkness just as a gun barked and a bullet whistled past his ear. It took three steps to get out of the light and behind a tree, and bullets followed each step.

When he got into the pitch darkness, Turner stopped and began the clumsy process of cocking the hammer back with one hand. The uselessness of his left arm and hand had almost cost him his life. His shirt was torn where Pickett's bullet had plowed through it. It was ironic, Turner thought, that he and Lemual had often practiced fanning the hammer back with the edge of the left hand so they could fire the gun rapidly. All that practice was for nothing now. Or was it? It had made him an expert with the old .44, and Shorty and Pickett must have been surprised that a school teacher could shoot so well. No, on second thought, they didn't have time to be surprised.

Now that the echoes had died, the only sound was the wind moaning through the tops of the tall ponderosas. Keiger was out there in the dark. He was no fool. He wouldn't come running up to the campfire to see what had happened. He knew very well what had happened. He had wanted to kill Turner before, and he would be even more determined to kill him now.

Turner believed he could make his way in the dark back to where he had tied the gray gelding and get back to town. He could send the deputy sheriff for Keiger and the other two. That is, unless Keiger managed to catch a ride on a freight wagon or waylay some horseback rider and take his horse. He'd do that if the opportunity arose, Turner knew.

Keiger had to be dealt with. But how? There was no hope of finding him and shooting it out the dark. Daylight was at least five hours away. It would be a long cold wait, but Turner decided that that was what he had to do.

He hunkered down at the foot of a big ponderosa and tried to mentally prepare himself for an uncomfortable night. A plan began to take shape in his mind.

Keiger would want to leave the country as soon as possible. He probably didn't know the horses had been set free, and he would come back to the grassy meadow near the creek to look for them. He would be out in the open. The thing to do, Turner decided, was to get to some spot where he could see the meadow without being seen. That meant groping around in the dark again, and Turner had had enough of that. But what else could he do? Just sit there under a tree and wait? Wait for what? For two men to stalk each other in the woods, with the survivor being the one who spotted the other first?

No, Turner had only one advantage. He knew where the horses were supposed to be and he knew Keiger would go there to find them. If Keiger tried to find them in the dark, he would have to do a lot of walking around, and sooner or later he would get between Turner and that quarter of a moon.

Turner stood up and started walking cautiously downhill from the campfire. The fire had almost burned itself out and was putting out very little light. A low pine branch dragged at his shirt and at the gun on his hip. It occurred to Turner that the gun was fully cocked and could fire accidentally. He eased the hammer down with his right hand without removing the gun from the holster.

Turner stayed along the creek where the aspens grew thick, hoping Keiger would not sense his movement. He stopped every few steps and listened. All he heard was the wind in the trees.

When he got to a spot near where he believed the horses had been tied, he stopped and again sat on the ground under a tree. Until then he had been too excited to notice the cold, but now it crawled from the seat of his pants on the cold ground to his feet and fingers and up to the top of his head.

He clamped his jaws shut to keep his teeth from chattering, and waited.

At times he dozed, but only for a few minutes at a time. Always the cold woke him up, and he always awoke with a start, wondering if Keiger had discovered him and was sneaking up on him. Each time he awakened, he looked around and listened. The breeze was picking up, ruffling his hair and shirt, bringing even more chill to the air. The stars and the quarter moon were blocked out at times by swiftly moving clouds.

Daylight came slowly. Turner had dozed off in the dark and when he awoke with a start, he could see vaguely across the small meadow to the road. He strained his eyes but saw no signs of life. It was a cloudy morning, and a heavy, wet fog was rolling in from the west. Visibility would not be good at any time that morning. Turner wanted to stand, to straighten his knees, but he was afraid to move.

Keiger was out there with a gun, probably waiting for a movement of any kind to show him where Turner was. Turner sat still. His shoulder ached and his knees ached. Something had to happen soon.

He caught a movement out of the corner of his left eye. Or did he? Did something move over there? He waited, looking at a point to the right of where he sensed movement. It was back in the fog, whatever it was, back there where everything was shapeless and vague. There. It moved again. What was it?

Something was moving. One of the horses? It was low, too low to be a horse. A coyote? It was moving too slowly to be a coyote. It had to be Keiger.

With all his senses straining, Turner watched, afraid to blink. Slowly, his hand moved to the gun. And slowly, he thumbed the hammer back without lifting the gun from its holster.

The clicking noise the hammer made in the mountain quiet sounded like a firecracker going off.

The movement at Turner's left stopped. A clicking sound came from the direction.

It was Keiger and he too had cocked a gun. He had picked Turner out of the semidarkness and he was going to shoot.

Turner raised the pistol and sighted along the barrel. It was too far for a snap shot, and the target was only a vague shape. He had to take aim.

Two guns boomed at once.

A chip flew off the tree just above Turner's head. Had he been standing, he would have been hit. At the same time, Keiger let out a scream.

'Don't shoot. Don't shoot. I'm hit.

Don't shoot.'

Turner got to his knees and crawled around behind the tree, keeping it between him and Keiger. He strained his eyes, trying to see.

'Oh, God, don't shoot,' Keiger's screams had changed to moans. 'I've been shot, don't shoot me again.'

'Come forward,' Turner yelled.

'I cain't. My arm. I've been shot.'

Turner couldn't help feeling a small amount of pity for the man. He was probably lying there helpless, unable to get up. But it could be a trick. It could be a scheme to get Turner out into the open where he would be a better target. The man was a killer. He had had every intention of killing Turner just two days earlier, and if Turner hadn't been lucky, Keiger would have killed him.

'Crawl,' Turner yelled.

'I cain't.'

'Crawl or I'll shoot.'

'Wait. Wait, I'll—I'll try.'

The vague shape in the fog moved slightly. It moved again. 'My arm. I'm bleedin'. I'm bleedin' to death.'

'Get out here where I can see you.'

The shapeless form moved again. It

began to take shape. Keiger was walking on his knees. He had no gun that Turner could see. His right arm dangled lifelessly at his side.

'All right, stop. Don't move. Don't move a muscle, Keiger, or I'll put three more bullets into you.' Turner stood up, straightening his knees slowly, painfully. He kept the .44 aimed at Keiger, and walked to him.

CHAPTER THIRTEEN

Blood soaked Keiger's shirt just above the left elbow. Turner walked around him, looking him over carefully. Keiger's gun holster was empty.

'Where's your gun?'

'Back there,' Keiger nodded in the direction he had come from. 'My arm. I'm bleedin' to death.'

'Stay where you are. Don't move.' Turner walked back to where Keiger had been when the shooting happened. It took a full three minutes to find the gun. It was lying in the grass, wet with the early dew, where Keiger had dropped it. Turner went back to Keiger.

'All right, on your belly. Face down. I'll have a look at that arm.'

'You—you're not gonna shoot me?'

'If you make one wrong move, I'll scatter your brains all over this county.' Turner was surprised at how tough he was talking.

Keiger lay face down in the wet grass. The arm was bleeding badly. 'I'm gonna freeze here. Do somethin', will you?'

'Why should I? You tried to kill me.'

'I didn't—I wouldn't—I had to.'

'Why?'

'We was already in trouble with the law and that banker offered us enough loot to get out of town, go a long ways.'

'In what way are you in trouble? Did you kill my brother?'

Keiger raised his head and tried to turn over on his back. 'No. No. I swear. We—I had nothin' to do with that.'

'Lie still. Who did it?'

'I don't know. I swear I don't. I never killed nobody.'

'Why are you in trouble with the law?'

'My arm. I'm bleedin' to death. Help me.'

'Why should I? Why should I help a bully like you. The world would be better off without you. I ought to just leave you here to die.'

'No, don't. Help me and I'll tell you somethin'. I'll tell you somethin' you don't know.'

'What?'

'Will you help me?'

'We'll see.'

'It was the fire. Shorty started it.'

'You mean the fire in the recorder's building?'

'Yeah. That banker paid Shorty to start it. He broke in a winder and poured kerosene from a lamp on that desk and set it afire.'

'Why did George Kemp want that building burned?'

'I don't know. Said somethin' about some papers that had to be burned up.'

Turner squatted on his heels and thought it over. The courthouse fire was arson. He had suspected that but didn't know for certain. Now he was certain. And he was even more certain that the banker did not actually buy that mine.

And suddenly it came to him. Suddenly he knew what had happened. Yes, it all fit. The figures penciled on a tent wall. 20,000 X 4. Suddenly it all came together.

Turner stood up and looked down at Keiger. 'All right. You didn't kill my brother. Let's have a look at that arm.'

He holstered the .44, but left it cocked, then bent over and tried to tear Keiger's shirt sleeve with one. It was impossible. He tried to wriggle the fingers on his left hand and succeeded. Slowly, he slipped his arm out of the sling and tried to move it. He could move it but only with a great deal of pain.

It took both hands to tear Keiger's shirt sleeve to the shoulder. A small piece of bone protruded through the wound. It was obvious the bullet had hit the bone and shattered it. Blood was pouring out of the bullet hole.

Wincing with pain, Turner ripped the shirt sleeve completely off, intending to use it for a tourniquet. Where to tie it? Turner tried to remember his premedical courses. The nearest pressure point is just below the shoulder, he remembered. He probed with his fingers for the vein and found it. He managed to get the sleeve tied around Keiger's arm at the pressure point. He found a stick and used it to twist the tourniquet tight. The bleeding slowed, then stopped.

'Sit up,' he said to Keiger. Keiger sat up.

'Here's the situation. Your left arm is badly broken. This tourniquet will stop the bleeding or at least slow it down considerably. But you have to release the pressure periodically or your arm will die from a lack of blood circulation. You take hold of this stick and when you feel your fingers getting numb, loosen the tourniquet until you get some of the feeling back. Then tighten it. You have to keep doing that. Meanwhile, we have to get you to a doctor. Where is the nearest doctor? Canon City?'

'I—I think so.'

'All right, the best I can do for you is wait for a freight wagon going to Canon City and put you on it. You'll be weak from the loss of blood, but I don't think you'll die if we can get you to a doctor before night. And if you don't go into shock. Keep calm, Keiger. You have to stay calm.'

Turner stood up and looked toward the wagon road. The fog was getting thicker and a light drizzle had started. He picked up Keiger's gun and threw it back into a clump of willows. Then he scrambled up to the road.

He couldn't see more than thirty feet in

the fog, but if a wagon were near, he would be able to hear it. But then if a wagon left Cripple Creek at daybreak, it would be noon before it got to where Turner was standing.

He walked back to where the campfire had been, found the two dead men exactly where he had seen them last, felt for pulses and found none.

All he could do then was wait.

Turner climbed the hill above the road and found the gray gelding still tied to a tree. He mounted and rode down to Keiger. He pulled the saddle off the horse, searched the ground until he found one of the abandoned halters and stake ropes and put it on the gelding. The horse was happy to be able to graze.

It was about noon, Turner estimated, before he heard traffic on the road. He scrambled up and waited. It was four wagons, pulled by four-horse teams. Turner stood in the middle of the road and waited for them.

The driver of the lead wagon whipped out his six-gun and aimed it at Turner at the same time he pulled up his team. Turner stood still, in his shirt sleeves, a bandage dangling from his left shoulder, bareheaded, wearing city clothes.

'What in Sam Hill're you doin' here?' the teamster demanded. 'And what do you want? And don't make no funny moves. I got a gun on you.'

'I mean you no harm,' Turner said. 'I've got a wounded man down here, and he needs transportation to a doctor.'

'Wounded? How?'

'He's been shot.'

'Who in hell shot 'im?' The driver was lean and had a wool cap pulled down to his eyebrows. He wore jackboots and striped pants held up with suspenders. 'Listen, mister, if you're thinkin' of robbin' us, don't. We got four armed teamsters back here and we ain't carryin' nothin' anyway.'

Turner held his right hand shoulder high and let his left arm dangle. 'I mean you no harm. I'm just asking you to help a man.'

'Who in hell shot 'im?'

'I did. It was a fair fight and he is wanted by the law. But I can't let him die here.'

'Listen, mister, all we got's a check to buy some supplies. We ain't carryin' no cash.'

'This is no robbery. I'm merely asking you to help a man. The man is wounded and helpless. He can't do you any harm.'

The driver studied Turner's face a moment, then turned to the wagon behind him. 'Hey, Nub, come help this feller, will you? If I let go this team, they might leave the country.'

It took two men to get Keiger up to the road and settled in the back of the second wagon. 'When you get to Canon City, be sure to turn him over to whoever represents the law,' Turner said. 'Tell them this man is wanted by Deputy Sheriff Mitchell.'

'We'll do 'er,' said the teamster. He turned to Keiger. 'You just lay there and be quiet,' he said. He handed his pistol to the driver of the first wagon. 'Ain't takin' no chances of him grabbin' my gun,' he said.

Someone hollered, 'Gee up,' and the wagons moved, rumbling and rattling, on down the road.

Turner watched them until they were out of sight in the fog, then went for his horse. With one strong hand and one weak one, he got the gray gelding saddled and got mounted. Once on horseback, he put his left arm back in the sling. The pain seemed to be less severe that way.

'Let's lope,' he said to the horse. 'I've got a score to settle.'

In fact, he had two scores to settle.

It was turning dark again when Turner rode up to the stables. The stableman had evidently locked up the barn for the night, but he heard or saw Turner ride up and he came out of his nearby shack. 'Man, I was beginnin' to think I'd never see you again. Where you been? Not that it's any of my business, but the deputy sheriff was here yestiddy and today lookin' for you.'

After the saddle was pulled off and the gray gelding was turned loose in a feed lot, it searched the ground with its nose, looking for a soft spot to lie down on and roll. It grunted with the pleasure it got from scratching its sweaty back on the ground. Then, having rolled completely over twice, the horse got up, shook itself, went to the nearest feed bunk and buried its nose in hay.

'He's as glad to be back as I am,' Turner said. 'Did the deputy sheriff say what he wanted?'

'Naw. Just wanted to keep an eye on you for your own protection, he said.' The stableman looked Turner over. 'Man, you look like you tangled with a buzz saw. It's none of my business, but where you been?'

Turner suspected the stableman liked to gossip and wanted something juicy to talk

183

about. He didn't answer. But the stableman was right. He looked and felt on the verge of collapse. He hadn't eaten in about thirty-four hours and hadn't been in a bed for two days and nights. His shoulder hurt and his face stung.

'I'll see if I can find him,' Turner said, walking away on unsteady legs.

'He ain't in his office. I seen him get his horse and head for his place. It's only a mile from here. I'll go get him if you want.'

'I'd sure appreciate that,' Turner said. 'Tell him he's got two dead bodies to go after and another man nearly dead in Canon City.'

The stableman's face brightened. 'Sure, sure. What happened? So I can tell 'im.'

'I'll tell him,' Turner answered. Then on second thought he didn't want to hurt the stableman's feelings. After all, the stableman was doing him a favor. 'Those three men who beat me up. I caught up with them on the Canon City road. There was some shooting. I'm the only one who didn't get shot.' With that, Turner started for the hotel.

The dinner was a frontier meal. Steak fried in a skillet, with beans and fried potatoes. Turner was almost too tired to eat

184

and his jaw was still sore. He cut the meat with one hand, with the edge of his fork, preferring to leave his left arm in the sling. He forced his jaws to work, to masticate the food. He washed it down with gulps of strong coffee. He was thinking about that comfortable bed upstairs.

Deputy Sheriff Mitchell didn't wait for an invitation. He stomped directly up to Turner's table, pulled out a chair and sat. He pushed his hat back and demanded, 'What's this about some dead men?'

He listened as Turner told him what had happened. He kept quiet until Turner finished talking, but his face was getting dark with anger.

'Now what the humped-up hell made you think you could take the law in your own hands? Why didn't you tell me? I'm the law around here, and no greenhorn school teacher is gonna go shootin' up people in my end of the county.'

'It was purely self-defense.'

'You say. How do I know you didn't bushwhack 'em?'

Turner felt his face getting red too. 'Like my brother and his partner were bushwhacked? Go down there and look and you'll find all of them shot at me first. All

185

but Shorty, I guess it was, and he was pulling his gun. Go look and you'll find they died with guns in their hands. What are you so upset about? They were hired killers and they got killed.'

He leaned across the table, his face closer to the deputy's. 'Listen, if you want to take this matter to the judge, I'll be happy to go along. Is the judge still in town?'

The lawman was seeing something in the Kansan he didn't expect to see, a toughness he didn't know the school teacher had. He forced himself to relax. 'All right, son. If it's the three that beat you up and if you say they tried to kill you, I won't make a fuss about it. I'll have to get my part-time helper and a wagon and go after them bodies. And I'll have to go after Keiger.'

Deputy Sheriff Mitchell started to get up, then sat down again abruptly. 'Did you say hired killers?'

Turner drained his coffee cup before he answered. 'They said George Kemp hinted that he would pay them to make me disappear. Their way of doing that was to shoot me in the head and seal me up in an abandoned mine shaft.'

The lawman shook his head. 'I cain't believe that, son. I've known George Kemp since I came here. Hell, he loaned me the money to buy my place.'

'All I know is what I heard, Mr. Mitchell. I'm not making any accusations yet, but I know what I heard.'

The deputy sheriff stood up and looked down at Turner. 'I ain't arrestin' you, but the judge might want to conduct a hearing on how them two died.'

'Where is the judge staying?'

The deputy sheriff glanced upward at the ceiling. 'Upstairs. Room 202.'

'I'll tell him what happened right now. If there's going to be any legal action over this I want to know about it now.'

'I cain't speak for the judge, son, but there probably won't be anybody arrested for shootin' it out with them three. Hell, you probably done the world a favor.'

'I want to see the judge, anyway.'

Judge Topkah was wearing a long night shirt when he answered the door to his hotel room. He was obviously irritated at being disturbed. 'I've got office hours, young man,' he said in a sharp tone. 'If you have any business with me, see me in the morning.'

'This is urgent, your honor. I'm sorry to disturb you.'

'Can't it wait?'

'I guess it could, but I was hoping you would hear me tonight.'

The judge hesitated, then opened the door wider and stepped back. 'All right. But it had better be important.'

When Turner stepped inside, into the lamplit room, the judge stared at him, looking him over from the pistol on his hip to the bandaged shoulder to his badly skinned and scratched face. 'You look worse than you did the first time I saw you. What happened?'

Wearily, Turner sat on the one chair in the room while the judge sat on the edge of the bed, and told of the events of the last two days and nights. The judge listened and only nodded. When Turner finished his story, the judge allowed as how the West was not completely civilized yet and there were times when some things had to be settled with guns. 'But you made a mistake in not turning this over to the deputy sheriff,' he said.

'I don't trust the deputy sheriff, your honor.'

Surprise showed in the judge's face. 'What? What has he done to make you say that?'

'I have nothing substantial against him. It's just that, well, Mr. Joel Lancaster, one of the county's leading citizens, warned me to be wary of him, and the way things have happened, I—' Turner shrugged.

Judge Topkah studied the floor. 'I see.' He looked up. 'What things?'

'Honestly, your honor, all I've got are suspicions, but they are well-founded. And as for the banker, Mr. Kemp, I know, I repeat, I know he did not buy my brother's claim.'

'Have you any proof?'

'No, but I'll bet I know somebody who does.'

'Who?'

'The deputy sheriff.'

'Now wait. You can't make accusations like that without proof.'

'I want you to ask him. Get him under oath and ask him. Make him realize that if he lies, he'll be punished for perjury.'

'If he is involved in some kind of fraud, putting him under oath will not make him tell the truth. The punishment for perjury would be less severe than the punishment for fraud.' The judge sighed. 'However, do you want to sign a complaint?'

'Definitely.'

'All right. Come to my, uh, the deputy sheriff's office first thing in the morning. By the way, if Mr. Kemp didn't buy the claim what was the document that was signed and attested to?'

'What he bought was a quarter interest in the mine.'

Judge Topkah's eyebrows arched higher. 'Yes? What makes you think so?'

'The evidence is weak, but it figures, your honor. First, my brother and his partner would not sell that claim, uh, mine, for twenty thousand dollars. That was the amount seen to change hands and that is the amount Mr. Kemp said he paid.

'Second, they needed money to build a road, buy some machinery and begin mining. They intended to raise the money by selling a quarter interest.

'Third, the recorder's office was set afire. Oh yes, the man named Keiger admitted to me that one of his partners was paid by the banker to commit arson. And don't you think it strange, your honor, that only that portion of the building, the portion where such papers are filed, was destroyed by fire?'

Judge Topkah was silent a moment. 'You realize, don't you, that the evidence you have is purely circumstantial?' He stood up and paced the floor, head down, thinking. 'You may be able to prove arson. That is, if that man Keiger lives and can be brought back here for trial. That's a very important if. And if Keiger lives, it will be a while before he is well enough to bring back here. Then Mr. Kemp will only deny it. It will be his word against that of a known hoodlum. And, too, it might be hearsay. I'm not sure at this point that I could allow Keiger to testify to what someone told him. A smart lawyer might succeed in getting that kind of evidence thrown out, or in getting a conviction reversed because of that kind of evidence.'

The judge's words fell like a heavy weight on Turner. He was tired, so tired he feared he would stagger and fall. That bed looked so inviting he couldn't keep his eyes off it. 'What you're saying, your honor, is that despite everything that has happened, I still have not won. Are you saying a fraudulent banker has won, has bought himself a valuable gold-mining claim for twenty thousand dollars?'

'What I'm saying, young man, is you need some solid evidence. I can't convict a man of fraud on that kind of evidence.'

'Will you question the deputy sheriff?'

'If you sign a complaint, yes.'

'I'll sign it first thing in the morning.' Turner stood up and walked out of the room without saying goodnight and without looking back.

He went to his own room down the hall and fell face down on the bed, fully dressed. One minute later, he was sound asleep.

*　　*　　*

The deputy sheriff was not in when Turner dropped into his office next morning. Turner was rested but sore, and his shoulder still ached. He had shaved the best he could and put on the last change of clothing he had with him. He still wore the gunbelt and gun. He turned and started to leave when he saw Judge Topkah coming. He waited.

'Good morning, young man,' the judge said. 'Is the deputy in?'

'No, your honor, I expect he went after the two bodies. If he did, he'll be gone most of the day, if not all day.'

'I see. Well, I can't conduct court without the deputy sheriff. Wonder if the fish are biting. Looks like it's going to clear up outside. Going to be a beautiful day.'

'Yes it is. After the cloudy, cold day yesterday, we could use some sunshine.'

'Think I'll try farther down the creek today. Caught two yesterday afternoon and had the cook at the Bluebird prepare them for my breakfast. Nothing better than fresh trout for breakfast. You ought to get in some fishing yourself before you leave here, young man. It's good for what ails you.'

'I'll, uh, I'll try to,' Turner said.

Turner went to the stable and was told the deputy sheriff took a light wagon and a light team and he and his helper drove off toward the Canon City road.

The morning sun felt wonderful, and Turner sat on a bale of hay for a while and enjoyed it. But the problem would not leave him, not even for a little while, and he tried to think of something he could do to alleviate it. That banker knows the answers, Turner mused. He and the deputy sheriff. They are no doubt the only ones who know exactly what happened.

Turner wondered what the banker's reaction would be if confronted with what he knew. George Kemp was a cold, calculating man, and he probably wouldn't

193

crack under any kind of accusations. But, Turner stood up, it was worth a try. He had to do something. He couldn't just sit and do nothing. And he had already decided he was not going to leave town until the truth came out, one way or another.

He was on his way to the bank when he met Mrs. Mahoney on Bennett Avenue. She was wearing a long dress with the usual ruffles at the collar and sleeves. Her dark hair was coiled at the back of her head. The dress fit snugly in places, and she was slender and shapely. She smiled, only the second time Turner had seen her smile. He was reminded again of what a pretty young woman she was.

'They told me at the hotel that you came back last night,' she said. 'I'm glad to see you. I was very worried.' A crease appeared between her eyes when she noticed the gun on his hip.

As usual, Turner was somewhat bashful in the presence of the pretty widow. 'I, uh, I had a chore to do. I didn't expect it to take two days, but it did.'

Her smile faded and she was serious. 'Does it have anything to do with the mine and the murders?'

'Yes, it did. It was—' He wanted to tell

her, to blurt it out. He had killed two men and possibly a third. What would she think? Would she ever talk to him again? He wanted her to think well of him. It was very important that she think well of him.

In a low and hesitant voice, he told her. 'There was some shooting. I, uh, am the only survivor. They tried to kill me a couple of days ago but I escaped. I went after them. It was a fair fight. I planned to shoot them down without warning, and I could have, but I didn't. They shot at me too.'

'Are you hurt? Is your shoulder any better? Oh, your poor face.'

Turner was stammering now like a schoolboy. 'You—you aren't displeased with me? I didn't intend, well, yes I guess I did, to shoot it out with them. I didn't know I had it in me.'

She spoke calmly. 'Don't worry about what I think, Mr. Turner. I know this is untamed country. My husband warned me about that. And as my husband has said, a man does what he has to do. You're a nice man. You've proved that.'

He fell in love with her then. He knew it. He couldn't help it. She was one in a million. One in a billion. If only he . . . But that was impossible. He had nothing to offer and she was a new widow. It was impossible.

She sensed that he wanted to say more but couldn't find the words. Puzzled, she said, 'It's not over yet, is it? Nothing has been solved.' The last words were a statement, not a question.

'No,' he answered. 'I know what happened. Your husband and my brother didn't sell their mine. They sold a quarter interest in it. But I don't know if I can prove it.'

'Will there be more shooting?' She glanced again at the gun on his hip.

'I don't know. Not if I can help it.'

'I don't want you to get hurt again. Your health, your life, is worth more than anything else.'

They were silent a moment, wrapped in their own thoughts. Then she touched his bandaged arm. 'But I know enough about you now to know you won't run from danger. You'll do what you think you have to do.' She turned to go. 'I won't leave until I know what has happened.' And then she turned back and looked into his eyes. 'Please don't take any more chances.'

Turner stood there on the boardwalk and

watched her walk away. He stood there a long time.

He was the center of attraction again as he walked through the bank lobby to George Kemp's office. Mr. Kemp was not in, a woman employee said. Mr. Kemp went out to one of his mines to oversee the installation of some new machinery, the woman said. The mine was just south of the town limits, within easy walking distance. It was called the Jackass Mine. Turner had no trouble finding it.

He could see the headframe from Bennett Avenue and a huge pile of low-grade ore that had been hauled out of the mine and dumped on the side of a steep hill. The dump was held up by woven wire supported by three thick timbers, which, if moved, would allow tons of crushed rock to tumble down into an arroyo.

The huge pulley on the headframe was turning, and soon an ore bucket appeared out of the mine. Two men emptied it into an ore car on the rails, then pushed the car out on top of the dump and emptied it. Some of the rock dropped into the arroyo.

The two miners stopped what they were doing and watched Turner approach from the road leading up to the mine. He was still bareheaded, still wearing city clothes and still had his left arm in a sling. 'Good morning,' he said. They only stared at him.

'Do you know where I can find Mr. Kemp?'

One of them nodded toward a freight wagon being unloaded by another man. At first, Turner didn't see George Kemp, but then, by looking under the wagon, he saw a pair of legs in striped pants on the other side of it. He walked over. George Kemp didn't see him at first. He was busy studying an invoice on a clipboard. When Turner spoke, his head came up sharply.

'What are you doing here?'

'I want to talk to you, Mr. Kemp.'

George Kemp gave Turner an exasperated look. 'I think I have said everything I have to say to you, Mr., uh, Mr.—'

'Turner. Bill Turner. Brother of Lemual Turner. Remember?'

'Oh yes. Well, I'm sure we have nothing more to say to each other.' He went back to studying the invoice.

'I think we do, Mr. Kemp. You see, I know what sort of transaction took place between you, my brother and Mike Mahoney.'

George Kemp's head came up in surprise again. 'What in tarnation are you talking about?'

'You know what I'm talking about.' Turner stood with his feet apart, his right thumb hooked over the gunbelt. 'I'm talking about fraud and arson.'

The three miners had gathered nearby out of curiosity. At Turner's words, they looked at each other, then watched Kemp's face.

'You are just making that up,' George Kemp said, his voice rising.

Turner spoke calmly. 'No, Mr. Kemp, I'm not making it up. I've been told how the fire started in the recorder's office. You paid a man named Shorty to start it. You paid him to do it because you wanted all papers concerning that transaction destroyed.'

George Kemp's features fell slack. He took a step backward. The miners watched him, watched Turner.

'That's not true. You're lying.'

Turner took a step toward George Kemp. 'Shorty is ready to tell all about it.' He was bluffing, but he hoped that George Kemp had not heard about Shorty's death.

It didn't work. Kemp suddenly stood

199

straighter. His face twisted into a sarcastic grin. 'Now I know you're lying. Shorty is dead.'

'How do you know?'

'Deputy Sheriff Mitchell told me so. He has gone after the bodies of two men you murdered.'

The miners stared hard at Turner.

'You know it wasn't murder. The deputy no doubt told you about the gun fight, a fair fight. And by the way, do you and the deputy sheriff consult each other every morning?'

The miners were now staring at George Kemp.

'We passed on the street. I make it a point to keep up with what is happening.'

'And the deputy sheriff told you all about it, did he? If he had thought it was murder, I would be in jail, isn't that right?'

'He wasn't convinced that what you told him was the truth.'

'Now you're lying, Mr. Kemp. Did the deputy sheriff tell you also about the message we found in the tent?' Turner was trying another bluff.

Kemp's eyes narrowed. 'What message?'

'Oh,' Turner said, his voice sarcastic now, 'he didn't report to you about that?

I'm talking about a note I found in the tent that said the partners were selling you a quarter interest in the mine.'

'You're lying again,' Kemp said. But he appeared to be less sure of himself.

'It's as plain as anything,' Turner persisted. 'It multiplied twenty thousand by four, which means they were figuring out what you thought the total value of the mine was. Any fool knows the mine was worth more than twenty thousand dollars.'

Kemp was on the defensive now. 'I paid a fair price. I didn't know for certain that I was buying a good mine. I was taking a gamble.'

'Samples assayed out at two hundred dollars a ton,' Turner said. 'I checked with the assayer on that. What you bought was a quarter interest to give my brother and Mike Mahoney some working capital. That's all you bought and that's all you're going to get.'

CHAPTER FOURTEEN

Kemp's eyes were darting from his miner employees to Turner and back. He licked his lips nervously. 'You're just making this up. You can't prove anything.'

Sensing victory, Turner kept pushing. 'It's very plain, Mr. Kemp. You bought a quarter interest in their mine. Someone murdered them for the money. When you heard about the murders, you saw a chance to get the entire mine for yourself.'

Kemp interrupted him, blurting out, 'I had nothing to do with those murders. Nothing.'

Turner ignored the outburst. 'You deliberately waited until Mrs. Hankins was closing for the day, then took the notorized purchase papers to her, talked her into putting them in a desk drawer without reading them, and then had Shorty set fire to her office.'

George Kemp took another step backwards. The miners were watching him.

'It just can't be a coincidence,' Turner persisted. 'Why else would only one half of the interior of that building be destroyed by fire? And isn't it very strange that Mrs. Hankins' desk was completely charred? It was a planned fire, Mr. Kemp. You told Shorty exactly what you wanted burned up. In a city with modern arson detection techniques, you couldn't have gotten away with it. Here, you almost did.'

George Kemp's mouth was working but no words came out. Turner stepped toward him, his hand close to the gun butt. Kemp turned to his employees.

'Stop him. He's going to shoot—murder me.'

'No, I'm not going to shoot you, Mr. Kemp. I'm going to make a citizen's arrest. I want to take you before Judge Topkah.'

'You can't prove this. You can't prove a thing.'

'Yes I can. Shorty is dead, but Keiger knows. And there's another man who knows all about it. Deputy Sheriff Mitchell.' Turner was bluffing again. It worked.

George Kemp's features fell. He screamed at his employees. 'Stop him.'

'Not me, Mr. Kemp,' said one of the miners. 'Everybody knows you got this mine from poor old starving Charlie. And we all know you had the deputy sheriff run 'im out of town so he couldn't talk about it.'

Another miner spoke up. 'Me neither. I don't owe you a damn thing, Mr. Kemp. You're the hardest man in El Paso County to work for. And the chintziest.'

The banker was frantic now. He turned and started down the road, but the three miners stood in his way. They made no threatening gestures, but they stood their ground. Kemp turned again and started downhill, toward the arroyo.

'Just wait till the deputy sheriff gets back,' he shouted over his shoulder. 'I'll see you all in jail.'

'I won't use force if I don't have to,' Turner said to the miners. 'I just want to make sure he doesn't leave town before the judge gets back from his fishing trip.' One of the miners nodded in agreement, and Turner followed George Kemp.

The hill was steep and the green grass made it slippery. George Kemp was half walking and half sliding. He grabbed at the grass with his hands to keep his balance. At one point, his feet slipped out from under him and he slid on his side a ways before he reached a level spot. Turner was also having a hard time keeping his feet under him. His bad arm made it even more difficult.

The banker was circling under the mine dump now, grabbing at everything he could reach to keep his balance. Turner saw the danger and shouted a warning. Kemp kept going. His feet slipped and he grabbed hold of one of the timbers. The timber shifted.

At first only a few rocks poured down, but then the whole dump moved. Kemp looked up and screamed.

The scream was choked off as tons of shattered rock fell into the arroyo. It completely buried the president of The New Gold District Bank.

*   *   *

'Why in hell did they have that rock propped up like that anyway?' It was Deputy Sheriff Mitchell asking.

'Aw, he said the price of gold would go up someday and he wanted it where he could haul it to the mill,' answered one of the miners.

The three employees of the Jackass Mine had gathered voluntarily in the deputy sheriff's office to tell how George Kemp died.

'Well that beats everything,' the deputy said. 'Why would he do something so stupid as to grab hold of a timber that was holdin' up all that rock?' The deputy sheriff had just got back to town with the bodies of Shorty and Pickett. It had been a long ride in a bouncing wagon, and his face revealed weariness.

'He was terrified,' said Bill Turner. 'I had confronted him with the truth about fraud and arson, and was threatening to take it to Judge Topkah. He was running.'

'What truth?' Mitchell had his hat pulled down and deep lines were etched in his face.

'The truth about how he had bought only a quarter interest in that mine and how he paid Shorty to set fire to the recorder's building.'

Judge Topkah entered the office, somewhat breathlessly, wearing a slouch hat and a wool shirt. 'What's this I hear about George Kemp getting killed?'

Nodding toward the miners, the deputy asked them to repeat their story. They did.

The judge sat down and shook his head negatively. He looked up at Turner. 'Why didn't he take the road? Why did he have to walk under those rocks anyway?'

'He was terrified,' Turner repeated. 'These men stood in his way. They did not threaten him, but they did refuse to take his side. I think George Kemp was afraid of nearly everyone. He was a crooked man and has apparently mistreated other people.'

'That's hard to believe.' Judge Topkah shook his head negatively again. 'A man like that. President of the local bank, a man of prestige.'

'He was greedy. He was rich and he wanted to get richer.'

'Now there's nothing wrong with being rich, and not every rich man is a crook,' the judge said.

'There is nothing wrong with getting rich,' Turner agreed. 'But it was the way he got rich. He made a practice of buying up promising mining claims for little money from hard-luck prospectors. The prospectors had no money to develop their claims and that made them easy pickings for George Kemp. He was a crook. Ask the deputy sheriff here.'

'What?' Mitchell was startled. 'Why ask me? How would I know?'

'You were in the bank when my brother and Mike Mahoney signed an agreement with George Kemp. You know what the agreement was. After the two partners were murdered, only you and George Kemp knew. Until now, that is. Now I know.'

'You're crazy.' The deputy appeared to be incredulous. 'You're touched in the head.'

Turner could feel the conflict slipping away from him. He knew what had happened, and he knew the deputy knew, but he still couldn't prove it. If George Kemp had not died, he might have been able to play him against the deputy and vice versa. But the deputy was a hard case. He feared no man.

Judge Topkah cleared his throat and looked from Turner to Mitchell. 'I see a long legal battle ahead,' he said. 'It will be the most interesting litigation in the state this year. There will be lawyers from Denver and Colorado Springs here to listen.'

He looked at Turner, at the three miners and back to the deputy sheriff. Was that a wink, Turner wondered, or just a twitch of the eyelid?

'You all will be called upon to testify,' the judge went on. 'It will take months for each side to prepare their case. There will be motions and counter motions. Winter will set in and the roads will be blocked with snow, creating delays. The hearing could go on all winter. Yes sir, it will make legal history, and I will be the presiding judge. I tell you, gentlemen, I will see that the truth comes out and justice is done.'

'All winter?' An outraged Deputy Sheriff Mitchell jumped to his feet. 'No sir, by God. I ain't stayin' another winter in these damn mountains. Justice be damned. I ain't freezin' my butt off another winter around here. I'm goin' back to Texas, by God.'

'If you do,' Judge Topkah said, 'you'll be brought back here under guard.' He glanced at everyone present. 'You'll all be here when court convenes, or gentlemen, the punishment will be severe. That is,' the judge said, looking at Turner, 'if Mr. Turner here presses his case. I happen to know George Kemp's sister in Colorado Springs—Mrs. Willoughby, her name is— and I'll bet my best fishin' rod she'll go to court. If she wins, she wins a gold mine. Yes sir, I just know she'll hire the best lawyer in the state.'

Deputy Sheriff Mitchell was pacing the floor. Turner had not seen him so nervous. His face was red and he looked as if he could explode. 'No sir, I ain't spendin' another winter here. I'm resignin' my job and hightailin' it back to Texas. Back to where a man can spit without havin' it freeze before it hits the ground.' He stopped in front of the judge. 'What if— what if I told you right now all about that transaction in the bank? Mr. Turner was right. I was there and I know what happened.'

A calm Judge Topkah looked up at the sheriff. 'What do you want to tell me, Mr. Mitchell?'

The lawman lifted his hat, ran his fingers through the thick gray hair and put the hat back in place. 'It was like Mr. Turner said. George Kemp bought a quarter interest in that mine. Lem Turner and Mike Mahoney told me they guessed they'd sell a quarter interest to him. Said they'd rather do business with Joel Lancaster, but he was down to Colorado Springs and wasn't expected back for a week or more. Said they wanted to get started buildin' a road and takin' ore out of that hole.'

'Why didn't you mention this before?' Judge Topkah asked. 'Don't you know you could be charged with being an accessory?'

'Hell, I'm no accessory.' The lawman's face was redder. 'I had to keep shut. George Kemp held the mortgage on my property, my cabin, my land, cows, horses.

Everything. He said he could foreclose anytime, and he could too.' The deputy's voice dropped an octave. 'It don't matter now. The board of directors'll foreclose. I've done lost everything.'

'But,' said the judge, 'you were planning all along to go back to Texas.'

'Sure. George Kemp promised he would buy my interest in the place. Ain't worth much, but it'd be enough to get me back to where I come from. Now I guess I'll have to leave here with nothin' but a few bucks in deputy wages.'

Turner had been keeping quiet, letting the judge do his talking for him. Now he spoke again. 'What do you think, your honor? With what you just heard, will there be a lawsuit?'

No answer came from the judge for a while. He was deep in thought. The only sound was a shuffling of feet by the three miners. When the judge spoke again, he measured his words carefully.

'I don't know. What I just heard will certainly pull a lot of weight. But who knows what some fee-hungry lawyer will do. A little more evidence might clinch it.'

'How about Keiger?' It was the lawman who spoke. 'I met those teamsters coming back from Canon City and they said Keiger was alive and bellyachin' when they delivered him to the marshall. He was in on that arson. Now that I think of it, it wasn't just Shorty, like Keiger told Mr. Turner here. I remember seein' him and Shorty walkin' away from the recorder's building just before somebody hollered fire.'

'Why didn't you think of this before?' the judge asked.

'Why should I? It wasn't till Bill Turner told me what Keiger told him that I remembered. If Shorty started that fire, Keiger was in on it. He'll spill his guts. You can tell your Mrs. Willoughy that. That'll clinch it.'

'Yes,' Judge Topkah stood up slowly and stretched. 'Yes, I believe that would do it. Young man,' he directed his words at Turner, 'I believe you just won your case. When I tell Mrs. Willoughby what I just heard, I believe she'll be happy to settle for a quarter interest in that mine.'

'Do I have to stick around here?' the deputy asked. 'Can I go back to Texas?'

'Mr. Mitchell,' the judge said, 'I ought to have you arrested for being an accessory. But under the circumstances ... well, you'd better wait until I present the case to

Mrs. Willoughby. If she accepts a quarter interest, then the whole matter is settled as far as I am concerned. Now, gentlemen, it has been a long day.'

The judge left.

CHAPTER FIFTEEN

This time it was Bill Turner knocking on Mrs. Mahoney's door. She had been brushing her dark hair and when she opened the door it was hanging straight down to her shoulders and she still held the brush in her hand. She was pleased to see him and her voice showed it.

'Mr. Turner. I'm glad you're all right. I heard about the accident at the mine and how Mr. Kemp died. Won't you come in?'

Turner entered her room and stood awkwardly, first on one foot and then the other. But he was happy. He had good news. 'We won, Mrs. Mahoney. It's our mine. Three-quarters of it is. And it's worth a lot of money.'

She inhaled sharply, eyes wide. 'Really?' How—what—was it the way you said? That Mr. Kemp only bought a quarter interest?'

'Yes ma'am. We got the deputy sheriff to admit he knew it all along. And the deputy says now he believes the fire in the recorder's building was arson.'

'We?'

'Yes. The judge and I. I had Kemp so scared he ran from me and got himself killed. But it would have been for nothing if the judge hadn't scared the deputy sheriff.'

'But,' she said, looking into Turner's eyes, 'I had the impression that nothing could scare Deputy Sheriff Mitchell.'

'He's a strange man,' Turner said. 'I doubt anything else would scare him other than the thought of having to spend another winter here in the cold mountains away from his beloved Texas. The judge gave him a story about a trial that would go on all winter unless some strong evidence surfaced.' Turner was chuckling. 'The deputy sheriff suddenly remembered some things he had not mentioned before.'

'Why that's wonderful, Mr. Turner.' She smiled again. It was the prettiest smile Bill Turner had ever seen.

'We ought to celebrate.'

Her smile faded and she looked

down. 'Oh, I'm sorry, Mrs. Mahoney. I'd forgotten. Of course you don't feel like celebrating.'

Silence engulfed the room. Turner could feel it. He shuffled his feet, trying to think of something to say. She broke the silence.

'It's all right, Mr. Turner. You have every reason to be elated. Had it not been for you, Mr. Kemp would have gotten one hundred percent of a gold mine for twenty thousand dollars, and you—we—would have received nothing. It was your persistence and the way you risked your life that won out. Whatever I get for my share of the mine I owe to you.'

'Oh no. You don't owe me anything. I—I'm sorry the way things turned out for you.'

She glanced at the gun on his hip. 'Is it over now, Mr. Turner?'

He didn't answer for a time. He shoved the gun aside and put his good hand deep into his pocket. 'No, I'm afraid it's not over yet. There is still a double murder to be solved. We have won a mine but the murders of my brother and your husband are still unsolved.'

'You can't do everything, Bill. Mr. Turner. Solving murders is the deputy sheriff's job. Why don't you leave that up to him, and leave with me on the stage tomorrow?'

Turner rubbed his sore shoulder. 'I hope to be on that stage,' he said. 'I've got to get this shoulder looked at. But there are a couple of things to do yet.'

He left and went down on the street.

The sun was moving close to the western horizon, but the street was still alive with wagons, buggies, men on horseback and men on foot.

Somewhere on a nearby hill a steam whistle tooted, signaling the end of the working day for one mining company's employees. Turner walked down Bennett Avenue. He heard his name called in a feminine voice and saw Rose Vandel waving to him from a buggy.

The buggy was pulled by a matched team of high-stepping bay horses.

'Congratulations, Bill Turner,' Rose Vandel yelled. 'I heard about it. It's all over town.' She leaned out of the buggy and looked back at him as the bays pulled the buggy past. 'Come down to the Spotted Pup and have a drink with me.' Her voice faded in the distance. 'One drink won't make you a drunkard.'

He smiled and waved. Sure, he said to himself. Why not? He walked faster and got to the Spotted Pup just as a man in rancher's clothing was helping her out of the buggy. It was Joel Lancaster. He tied the team to a hitch rail.

He was all smiles when he saw Bill Turner. He held out his hand and they shook hands heartily. He slapped Turner on the back. 'This drink's on me,' he said. He nodded toward the bandaged shoulder. 'Hope you didn't break anything. And what happened to your face? Looks like you tried to take dinner away from a bobcat.'

'I feel like it too,' Turner grinned.

They stood at the bar and Joel Lancaster ordered the bartender to set up a table for the three of them. Turner, unaccustomed to drinking, ordered a glass of beer. Rose Vandel and Joel Lancaster ordered whiskey.

'That's a fine looking team you've got out there,' Turner said to Rose Vandel. 'Business must be booming.'

With a broad wink and a broad smile she tipped up her glass and drank its contents. Her smile changed to a wry face and back to a smile again. 'Like I said, Mr. Turner, lots of men are getting rich around here and so am I. Another year and I'll be going back to St. Louis. By the way,' she added, 'what did happen to your face?'

'I fell off a horse,' he quipped.

'Hey, mister.' It was a man in overalls and thicksoled shoes talking. 'Are you the feller that scared the pee-waddin out of ol' George Kemp?'

'He's the one,' Joel Lancaster answered.

The man smiled, showing dark teeth among a bushy beard. 'Well, I want to buy you a drink. I usta work for that jasper and I'm glad to hear he got buried in his own mine. He was nothin' more'n a claim jumper.'

Within ten minutes, four other miners offered to buy a drink for Turner. The Spotted Pup was full of miners just off the day shift, and the main topic of conversation was the death of George Kemp and how he had been thwarted in his attempt to obtain another mine for a small fraction of what it was worth.

Within ten more minutes, Turner was offered ten more drinks.

The beer Turner held in his hand was not as cold as it should have been and he didn't like the taste of it. He forced it down

218

anyway and looked for an excuse to leave.

'Gets kind of close in here, doesn't it?' said Joel Lancaster. He waved toward an unoccupied table against the far wall. 'Let's you and I sit over there. I've got a proposition for you.'

They worked their way through the crowd at the bar. Rose Vandel was having a good time joking with the miners and didn't see them leave. Joel Lancaster pulled out a wooden chair and sat, gesturing for Turner to do the same.

'You can't talk business in that mob,' he chuckled. 'Now,' he said as Turner took his seat, 'what do you think that mine of yours is worth?'

Several moments passed before Turner answered, then he talked slowly. 'It's not just my mine, Mr. Lancaster. It's Mrs. Mahoney's too. And George Kemp's sister's.'

'Yeah, I know. But they'll probably agree to any price you put on it.'

'I don't know. I haven't had time to think about it.'

'Take your time, but I'm going down to Colorado Springs tomorrow and if you want to go with me we can have the papers drawn up and I can make out a check right

219

there.'

Turner grinned. 'You people believe in doing business in a hurry, don't you?'

'No use dawdling. I've got two good mines and I can afford to buy another. Now, you're no miner and you no doubt would like to get back to Kansas City or wherever you came from. I'll pay you what your interest in the mine is worth, then dicker with Mrs. Mahoney and Mrs. Willoughby. Name a figure.'

'Let's see.' Turner's mind was working. 'George Kemp paid twenty thousand dollars for a quarter interest. He no doubt paid only half of what a quarter interest was worth. That would put a quarter interest at forty thousand dollars.' He looked Joel Lancaster in the eye. 'That would put the total value of the mine at one hundred and sixty thousand dollars, Mr. Lancaster.'

Joel Lancaster didn't hesitate a second. 'All right. Now. You say it's worth a hundred and sixty thousand. I don't agree, Mr. Turner. I'll give a hundred and ten.'

So that's the way horse traders work, Bill Turner thought.

Joel Lancaster persisted. 'Your share of a hundred and ten would be over forty-one thousand, Mr. Turner. You could live in luxury for a long time on that.'

Turner stroked his chin and thought it over. 'Not one cent less than one hundred and fifty-five thousand dollars.'

'All right. A hundred and twenty.'

'One hundred and fifty and that's final, Mr. Lancaster.'

Joel Lancaster shrugged and spread his hands. 'Let's quit dickering, Mr. Turner. Your brother and his partner worked hard for that mine. You fought hard and nearly lost your life for it. Mrs. Mahoney lost her husband and her son because of it. I don't blame you for not wanting to sell cheap. I won't dicker anymore. A hundred and forty thousand.'

He meant it, Turner believed. The horse trading was over. Turner believed it was as good an offer as he would ever get, and Joel Lancaster was right, he had no interest in mining. He held out his good right hand. They shook.

Joel Lancaster leaned back in his chair, pulled a long dark cigar from his vest pocket and lit it. 'This calls for another shot of booze,' he allowed. 'Today's events make me the biggest mine owner and the biggest landowner in this end of El Paso County.' He puffed on the cigar and blew thick smoke at the ceiling. 'And I came by it all honestly. I got lucky, Mr. Turner. My first mine, the Bluebird, started making money hand over fist immediately, and I used the proceeds to buy another, smaller mine. Now I've got yours and it looks like a winner. Cattle prices are up and I'm going to get top dollar for my fall beef gather. That enables me to buy more land and more cows. I just bought Deputy Sheriff Mitchell's place, everything but two horses. It isn't much, but it does add to my land inventory. And it gives Mitchell enough money to go back to Texas. Now, how about that drink, Mr. Turner?'

Turner didn't hear the question. He was deep in thought.

'Mr. Turner?'

'Oh,' Bill Turner said, his mind coming back to the present. 'I can still taste the last drink I had. I'm just not a drinker, I guess. What did you say about buying out Deputy Sheriff Mitchell?'

'Not more than an hour ago. Just before I met Rose Vandel on the street. Why?'

'I'm just curious, that's all. It's none of my business, Mr. Lancaster, but may I ask how much you paid him?'

'Two thousand for his equity. In cash. I

had to commit myself to paying off the mortgage on the property. I understand Mitchell has resigned his job and is leaving first thing in the morning.'

'I see.' Turner was deep in thought again.

'Are you going down to Colorado Springs tomorrow?' Joel Lancaster asked. 'I'm taking the stage myself to Florissant and the Midland Railroad the rest of the way. We can complete our transaction in my lawyer's office next day. I'll go and see Mrs. Mahoney tonight and see if she'll agree on the price you set. I'm betting she will. Then we can all three have a good dinner together in Colorado Springs tomorrow night.'

Turner was still pensive.

'Something wrong, Mr. Turner? Think she'll be stubborn?'

'What? Oh no. No, I don't think so. She doesn't know any more about gold mines than I do. She'll probably sell. It's just—let me ask you, Mr. Lancaster. If by any chance I don't get on that stage, if anything happens to me, will you do me a favor?'

'Name it.'

'Will you see that my folks get my share of the money. I'll write down their address

223

for you.'

'Why sure, but what—'

'I can't tell you anymore. It's just that I've got some more business to take care of.'

CHAPTER SIXTEEN

Daylight was still an hour away when Bill Turner knocked on Judge Topkah's hotel room door. He heard a muffled voice from inside say, 'Who is it?'

'Bill Turner, your honor. I have to see you.'

'Go away,' the muffled voice said.

'I'm sorry, your honor. I apologize, but this is very important.'

'Nothing is so important that we have to talk about it in the middle of the night.'

'Yes sir, it is. Can I come in?'

The judge was still not wide awake and his voice showed it. 'Why? What's all that important?'

'I can't tell you out here in the hall, your honor.'

'Go away.'

'I'm sorry, but I have to see you and I

have to see you now.'

'Oh, all right.'

Turner heard the bedsprings squeak, heard the judge mumbling to himself, heard footsteps. A dim light came on under the door and Turner knew the judge had lit the kerosene lamp. More grumblings and finally the door was opened a crack.

The judge's hair was mussed and his eyes were bleary. He wore a long night gown. 'What in the name of Job is the matter with you, young man? I've never seen nor heard of one man causing a jurist so much trouble. What is it this time?'

'May I come in? I can't tell you about it here in the hall.'

Stepping back a step, Judge Topkah opened the door wider. Turner entered and stood in the center of the room, facing the judge.

'It's about my brother's murder, your honor. I know who did it.'

Judge Topkah went to the washbasin, poured some cold water into it and splashed water on his face. 'Brr,' he said. He dried himself off with a towel. 'Now, what did you say? Something about a murder?'

'Yes, sir, my brother's and Mike Mahoney's. I know who did it but right now I can't prove it.'

Looking tired and resigned, the judge said, 'Well you don't need to come before a judge without proof. The court weighs evidence. We don't gather it. That's up to the law enforcement officers.'

'But, your honor, the killer is a law enforcement officer. That's why I need your help.'

'What?' the judge came awake. 'What do you mean? Deputy Sheriff Mitchell?'

'Yes, sir. And he is leaving first thing this morning. We have to be at his place by daylight or shortly after.'

'Why so blamed early? And you said you still have no proof.'

'Not now I don't. But if we can catch him in the act of leaving, I will have.'

'I repeat, why so blamed early? If he is leaving, the stage won't leave until nine in the morning.'

'He's going on horseback. He won't wait for the stage.'

'How do you know so much?'

'Because he sold his small ranch, his equity in it, to Joel Lancaster. All but two horses. He is no doubt planning to leave as soon as it's daylight.'

'Well, what do you want me for?'

'To be there when I uncover the evidence. I want you to witness it.'

'Young man, do you know what this would do to my career if you are mistaken? I'd be the laughing stock of the whole Colorado judicial system.'

'If I'm wrong, you can have me arrested for making false accusations, your honor. Or have me arrested for something.'

The judge started laying out his clothes on the bed. 'I can't go anywhere without my morning coffee. Now, if you'll excuse me, young man, I like to dress in privacy.'

'But the restaurant is not open yet, and we have to be there by daylight or shortly after.'

'How far is Mitchell's place?'

'About a mile out of town toward Canon City. We can walk.'

'As I said, young man, I like to dress in privacy.'

Turner left, closing the door behind him. He waited in the hall for about five minutes before the judge came out, dressed in outdoor clothes.

'You ought to wear something warmer, young man. It's mighty cool in these mountains before sunup.'

'I don't have anything else, your honor. I

227

came here unprepared for this sort of thing.'

'You're still carrying that gun. Do you need it? I've learned, young man, that he who carries a gun generally has to use it. Can't you leave that behind?'

'I wish I could, your honor, but I'm afraid . . .' Turner shrugged.

'All right,' the judge said. 'Let's go.'

A half moon created enough light that Turner and Judge Topkah could find the road and follow it. They stubbed their toes at times on the rocks and stumbled over the wagon ruts, but the judge walked right along. Turner was panting for breath, having a hard time keeping up with the judge.

'It's the altitude,' Judge Topkah said. 'I've lived around here long enough that I'm used to it, but strangers such as yourself find they have no wind.' He stepped right along. Turner huffed and puffed. 'No wind at all,' the judge said.

Daylight was beginning to seep upward around the horizon to the east. A coyote let out a series of excited yap-yap-yaps, letting his friends know he had a prey in sight and might need some help. Turner had lived on the Kansas prairie long enough to know coyotes would not attack a human, but he was not familiar with mountain coyotes.

'They're harmless,' the judge said.

Turner shivered, but it was because of the cold. It seemed he had spent half his life lately in the cold and the dark. He still had his left arm in a sling, simply because it was more comfortable that way, and it still ached at times. The shoulder definitely needs medical attention, he decided, and the sooner the better. If not soon, complications could set in. The gun on his hip was heavy. Would he really need it? If it came to shooting, he didn't have a chance against Deputy Sheriff Mitchell.

With the judge there, hopefully, the deputy wouldn't dare try to shoot his way out of trouble. On the other hand, the deputy had nothing to lose. Absolutely nothing. And he is a killer. No doubt about that.

The gun felt heavy on Turner's hip, but in a way it was comforting too. With it, he at least had a fighting chance.

They could see a mine headframe to their right now. The sky was becoming lighter. They walked on, Turner panting like a wind-broken horse.

'It was good of you to accompany me,

your honor.'

'Save your wind, young man. And if you can't prove your allegations, you are in serious trouble, I'll see to that.'

'Yes, sir.'

They topped a small rise and looked down in the dim light at Mitchell's one-room cabin and corrals. The country rose sharply to the south of the place.

'Humph,' the judge said. 'Anyone wise to the mountains knows better than to build a house on the north side of a high hill. If you do you'll never see the sun in the winter.'

As they walked closer, they could see a pole stock shelter at one end of the bigger of two corrals. It was enclosed on three sides and had a pole roof on it. A freight wagon stood in the yard. The yard sloped down to the creek that ran parallel with the road. A hitchrack had been built at the north side of the cabin, and two horses were tied to it.

Turner took hold of the judge's arm. 'Let's wait a minute,' he said, 'and see what he's up to.' The judge stopped. They stood on the road in the semidarkness and waited.

Mitchell came out of the cabin carrying a

cowboy bedroll. He sat it beside one of the horses and went to the stock shelter for his saddles. Turner and the judge squatted behind a boulder and watched. The deputy put his saddle on one of the horses, and a pack saddle on the other. He went back into the cabin, then returned with two canvas panniers. He distributed the groceries and cooking utensils in them, then lifted them one at a time to see if they were approximately the same weight.

He hung them one at at time over the crossbucks on the pack saddle, one on each side, then put his bedroll on top. He started to tie it all down with a lash cinch when Turner stood up.

'Let's go,' Turner said. The judge stood up too, and they walked across the bridge over the creek and approached the lawman.

Mitchell was so engrossed in throwing a diamond hitch over the pack that he didn't see them coming. That is, until the pack horse's head came up and its ears pointed toward them.

The deputy wheeled around in a crouch, his hand going for the pistol he carried in a low holster. He had the gun out and cocked before he recognized Judge Topkah.

'What,' he said, 'what in hell you doin''

out this early, Judge?' He straightened up and relaxed 'Lookin' for a fishin' spot?' He recognized Turner then and his eyes narrowed. 'What're you doin' here, son?'

When they didn't answer immediately and continued walking toward him, suspicion showed in his face. 'Somethin' tells me this ain't no social call. Suppose you stop right there and talk to me.'

They stopped, each wishing the other would say something. Finally Judge Topkah spoke. 'This young man seems to think you know more about his brother's murder than you're willing to tell. Mr. Mitchell.'

Mitchell's glance darted from the judge to Turner. 'Now what the humped-up hell're you talkin' about?' His hand hovered near the gun butt.

'I'm convinced now, Mr. Mitchell,' Turner said. He turned to the judge. 'I'm convinced that if you search his packs and his pockets you'll find the twenty thousand dollars George Kemp paid my brother and Mike Mahoney.'

Sputtering rage came from the lawman. 'Why you silly, eastern farmer, sodbuster, bookheaded, lyin'—Are you sayin' I killed them two?'

Turner watched the man's gun hand and knew he could be dead in a split second. Fear crept into his throat. 'Yes,' he said, trying to control his voice. 'Yes, that's what I'm saying.'

They faced each other for a long moment. Mitchell looked to be on the verge of drawing his gun. Turner was scared and trying not to show it. Then suddenly Mitchell ralaxed again. 'Aw, hell, Judge. You know by now this bookthumper is always accusin' somebody of somethin'. Only thing I'd like to know about him is how he's lived so long.'

The judge spoke again. 'Have you got twenty thousand dollars on you, Mr. Mitchell?'

'Sure, I've got some money. I sold my ranch here yestiddy to Joel Lancaster. He'll tell you about that.'

'How much did you sell it for?'

Mitchell's glance again went from the judge to Turner and back to the judge. 'Twenty-two thousand.'

Turner shook his head negatively. 'Not so. Joel Lancaster told me what he paid for your small equity in this property. It was two thousand dollars, and your honor, I'll bet he's got about twenty-two thousand

233

dollars on him.'

Face red with anger now, Mitchell hissed, 'You're a liar.'

No one spoke. Mitchell glared at Turner. Turner felt his stomach knotting with fear. He was no match for Mitchell and he knew it.

'Where I come from,' Mitchell hissed, 'when a man calls another man a liar, them's fightin' words. You ain't even a man.'

Trying desperately to fight down the fear and keep his voice calm, Turner took his eyes off Mitchell and turned to the judge. 'Didn't he tell us yesterday that the bank was going to foreclose on this place? He said George Kemp held the mortgage on it. That was no doubt true. But what George Kemp also held on him was knowledge of the murders. He, in turn, knew that George Kemp came by that mine through fraud and conspiracy. They blackmailed each other.'

'That's a lie. You're a liar.' The deputy spat in the dirt.

'Your honor,' Turner went on, his stomach churning, 'he is the second man in two days to call me a liar. The first one turned out to be a liar himself while I was telling the truth. When George Kemp was killed, Mitchell here was in the clear. He had no reason then not to tell what he knew about that banker. He told everything to keep from having to stay here for a long trial.'

The lawman hawked and spat a glob at Turner's feet. 'I'm callin' you a liar, schoolteach. What're you gonna do about it?'

Turner tried to ignore him.

'Now, gentlemen,' Judge Topkah said, 'let's not have any gun play.' His voice took on a pleading note. 'Please, no shooting. Let's talk this over calmly, shall we?'

In a voice shaking with anger, the man blurted out, 'What's there to talk about? This lily-livered school teacher here is callin' me a murderer.'

'Why,' the judge asked in a placating tone, 'did you tell us an untruth about how much you were paid for this ranch?'

'Hell, it's nobody's business what I was paid. It's nobody's damn business.'

'All right, all right,' Judge Topkah said. 'Let's see now. It seems to me, young man, you have reason to be suspicious, but no proof. You have to have proof, you know. You told me before I agreed to accompany you here that you had proof. Now where is it?'

Anger was seeping into Turner now, and it was driving away the fear. Mitchell was a good actor. Turner had been warned about that. He could appear to be a good fellow one minute and become a killer the next. He was putting on an indignant act and he was fooling the judge. 'It had to be him,' Turner said. 'He was in the bank when George Kemp paid my brother and Mike Mahoney twenty thousand dollars in cash. He knew they had the money in their pockets. He knew where they were going. It had to be him.'

'Hell,' Mitchell spat out, 'everyone knows by now that them three—Keiger, Shorty and Pickett—killed them two. They worked for George Kemp. They were his hired guns.'

'No.' Turner could see doubt in the judge's face. His voice rose. 'They didn't do it. If they had, they wouldn't have stuck around to do more of George Kemp's dirty work. They'd have left the country and gone some place where they could spend twenty thousand dollars without arousing suspicion.'

While he talked, Turner edged closer to

the lawman. He was angry now, but not so angry that he wanted to throw his life away in a fast draw contest with a man who made a speciality of it. 'He followed them to their claim, and when they saw him coming they had no fear of him because they knew he was a representative of the law. That made it easy.' Turner got closer.

'You're a goddam liar.'

Turner hit him. He brought his right fist up from hip pocket level and aimed at the lawman's chin. The blow landed with a loud smack.

Mitchell staggered back, tripped over his own feet and landed hard on his back. His hand went to the gun. At the same instant, Turner leaped forward and his left foot came down on the gun and Mitchell's hand. He stomped on the hand.

Cursing wildly, Mitchell let go of the gun and scooted back on the seat of his pants away from it. Turner reached down and picked up the gun.

The deputy recovered quickly. He scrambled to his feet and ran to his saddle horse, reaching for the rifle in the saddle boot. 'You're both dead,' he screamed, and added a string of obscenities. The horse skittered away and pulled back on the bridle reins.

The judge yelled, 'Take cover.'

CHAPTER SEVENTEEN

Both men ran, bent low, for the stock
shelter and got behind it just as Mitchell
got the rifle free and jacked a cartridge into
the firing chamber. The rifle fired and a
bullet knocked chips off the pole shelter
near where Turner and Judge Topkah
crouched.

'Hit the ground,' Turner said. 'Flatten
out.'

Judge Topkah dropped onto his hands
and knees, then onto his belly.

Another shot came from the rifle. The
bullet found its way between two poles on
the shelter and sang a deadly song over
Turner's head before it embedded itself in a
pole on the opposite side.

Turner took his left arm out of the sling.
It hurt, but he barely noticed it. He held
Mitchell's pistol in his left hand and drew
the .44 with his right hand. He cocked the
hammer back.

'He's got us pinned in here,' Turner

said. 'He can't see us, but if he keeps shooting, a lucky shot will hit one of us sooner or later.'

'Oh, my God,' Judge Topkah muttered. 'Oh, my God.'

Pow went the rifle. *Thunk* went a bullet into the pole structure.

Turner flattened out on his stomach. Slowly, he crawled forward. He knew he had to have a look around the corner of the structure, and he knew he would be a good target when he did. But he couldn't just cover his head and let Mitchell shoot at will. Keeping his face only a few inches above the ground, Turner crawled forward another foot and peered around the corner. The lawman was not in sight.

'He'll kill us both,' the judge moaned.

Turner raised up onto his hands and knees. His left shoulder hurt. Where is he? Turner asked himself. What's he doing? He caught a movement out of the corner of his left eye. It was only a blur. Then it was gone behind a boulder. It had to be Mitchell. He was circling to where he could get a clear shot. 'My God,' Turner said, 'he's getting out there where he can pick us off and we won't even know where he is until we've been hit.'

239

Turner flattened out again, but kept his head up. He had to keep his eyes alert. Movement again. Mitchell's booted feet and legs came into view under the bottom corral pole in front of the stock shelter. They were running. Turner aimed the .44 and fired. The feet kept running until they disappeared behind a rise in the ground.

'Now he's got us,' Turner said aloud. 'He's over there in a gully where he can see into this shed. If he gets a chance to take aim, he can't miss.'

'We're going to die,' Judge Topkah moaned.

Mitchell's head and shoulders appeared above the rise. Turner snapped a shot. The head and shoulders disappeared. Got to keep him down, Turner thought. Can't let him take aim. The head appeared again and Turner snapped another shot. He saw the bullet kick dirt in the Texan's face, and saw the face drop behind the rise.

'We're not going to make it easy for him,' Turner said to the judge. 'But we have to get out of here. Sooner or later, he'll rise up some place where I don't see him and it'll be all over.'

He was afraid to take his eyes off the rise, but he had to look around and find a better shelter. The freight wagon in the yard. It was too far. But he had to get out of the bed. He was too good a target there. Movement. He snapped another shot at Mitchell's head, knew he had missed, but hoped it would keep the man's head down long enough for him to run for the wagon. He ran.

Bending low, carrying both pistols, Turner ran for his life. The rifle barked and a bullet hit the ground by his left foot. Run, Bill Turner, he told himself. Do it like the Indians do. Run zigzag. He turned left and turned right. Another bullet went past his ear. He reached the wagon. A bullet thunked into the side of it. He jumped over the wagon tongue and half fell on the other side. He stopped, panting hard. Another bullet hit the ground near his feet. He knew then his feet and lower legs were exposed. Quickly, he scrambled into the wagon.

For a moment he lay there, trying to catch his breath. He noted with satisfaction that the bullet that hit the side of the wagon did not penetrate it. At least the judge was safe now, he thought. The gunfire would all be directed at him.

The saddle horse, spooked by the gunfire, had broken its bridle reins and was running across the yard. The pack horse, tied with a strong halter and rope, was rearing back, trying to break loose. Another bullet hit the side of the wagon. Then for a few minutes, all was quiet.

Turner figured the deputy had grabbed a box of cartridges when he grabbed the rifle, and was reloading. It occurred to Turner that he and the lawman were in a standoff then. He was protected by the wagon, and the Texan was in his gully. The winner would be the luckiest, Turner thought. One of them would dare to look up, get up and approach to where he could get a clear shot. Either he would succeed or get shot trying. If he didn't want to be the daring one, Turner knew he at least would have to look up now and then and keep Mitchell from being the daring one.

He raised his head cautiously, and ducked immediately when he saw a puff of smoke from the rifle. The bullet went over his head at the same instant the rifle barked.

Strangely, Turner felt no fear. He was in a deadly game, he knew. But for some reason he couldn't understand, he was calm. He had been shot at before in the past few days. He had been hunted, and he had been the hunter. Too much had happened. He was becoming accustomed to danger. So much had happened.

He had to look around. He couldn't just stay there in the wagon with his head covered up. Something had to give. He readied the .44 and raised his head. He saw Mitchell snap a shot in his direction and he returned the fire. Mitchell ducked. Both shots were hasty ones and both missed.

At least, Turner thought, he's as much afraid of me as I am of him. The rifle is more accurate but the pistol is quicker. Let's see. Five shots. One more in the cylinder.

With the pistol handy on the wagon floorboards, Turner took cartridges out of his gunbelt and filled the cylinder of the .44.

Two quick shots came from the deputy and thudded against the wagon. What's he doing? Turner wondered. And then he knew. The Texan had fired to keep his head down, the same way Turner had tried to keep the Texan's head down. Mitchell was moving.

Turner raised up just in time to see Mitchell duck behind a ponderosa uphill from him. That's it, Turner thought. If he can get high enough on that hill, he can shoot down into the wagon. I've got to move again. How?

He remembered the wagon was parked on a grade, headed down toward the creek. If he could release the brake, the wagon would roll.

Turner crawled forward under the wagon seat and reached up for the brake handle. A bullet screamed off the iron handle inches from his hand. He jerked his hand back, then cautiously reached for the brake handle again. He couldn't move it. He knew he would have to pull it toward him, then push it forward. He remembered that teamsters did that with their right feet. He didn't have enough strength in his one hand and he forced himself to raise his left arm and get his left hand on it. With both hands he pulled and pushed. His left shoulder hurt.

The brake was released and the wagon started to roll.

It moved slowly at first, then gradually picked up speed. Creaking and banging, it went downhill, moving eventually at a good clip. The wagon tongue was being pushed along the ground ahead. It plowed a small furrow.

Turner felt as if he was riding in an

armored wagon, but one he could not steer. The wagon turned left, turned back to the right again. It bounced over rocks. Then the tongue met head on with a large boulder.

The impact raised the rear wheels off the ground. The wagon veered sharply and turned over on its side. Turner was spilled out, scooting on his stomach, rolling. Searing pain went through his left shoulder. He groaned. A rifle bullet hit a rock near his head and went spanging off toward town.

He rolled behind the boulder, the one that had caused the wreck. His shoulder hurt so bad he was dizzy with pain. He sat up and shook his head, trying to clear his mind. A bullet richocheted off the boulder. He saw that he had dropped his guns. Mitchell's pistol was out in the open, but his .44 was behind the wagon.

Bill Turner left the shelter of the boulder and jumped behind the overturned wagon. He grabbed up the .44 and looked over the top.

Mitchell was running. He was ducking behind trees, but he was coming downhill. He ducked behind a tree and fired again. The bullet hit the wagon. Then he was running again, right toward Turner, firing and working the lever on the rifle as he ran, keeping as many trees between him and the wagon as he could. Another bullet hit the wagon, and splinters appeared on the inside, on Turner's side. The man was close enough now that his bullets were penetrating the plank sides of the wagon.

Turner guessed what Mitchell had in mind. He was no doubt hoping that Turner had been hurt when the wagon turned over. He knew that Turner had been able to move from behind the boulder to behind the wagon, but he was hoping that Turner was injured enough that he could not put up much of a fight. He was hoping but he was not sure. He was not willing to make a good target of himself until he knew for sure.

Turner cocked the .44 and waited until the next shot hit the wagon, then stood up. He saw the deputy duck behind a tree. He took careful aim, sighting down the short barrel of the gun. The deputy's head and right arm and hand, holding the rifle, appeared from behind the tree. He was ready to shoot again. Turner squeezed the trigger.

The lawman jerked around and fell onto

his knees, dropping the rifle.

Turner vaulted over the wagon and ran toward him. Mitchell was walking on his knees. He was headed toward the fallen rifle. He picked it up with his left hand.

Turner fired while running and the bullet hit the ground harmlessly. Mitchell held the rifle with one hand and fired. The bullet went past Turner. Mitchell tried to raise his right arm but couldn't. He levered another cartridge into the firing chamber with his left hand, holding the stock of the rifle on the ground between his knees. He raised the gun one-handed again.

Turner had stopped and was taking aim. The .44 boomed and bucked.

Mitchell pitched forward onto his face. It was the last thing he ever did.

CHAPTER EIGHTEEN

At first, Turner couldn't believe it. He climbed the hill to where Mitchell lay and looked down at him. The man was breathing in noisy ragged breaths. His breathing slowed, then stopped.

Fear caught up with Turner then. With a

shaking hand, he holstered the .44. Fear was in his stomach. It surged into his throat with cold fingers. He shook with fear. He dropped onto his knees beside the dead man.

'How many?' he asked himself aloud in a pained voice. 'How many men have I killed?'

He squeezed his eyes closed and moaned.

Several minutes passed before Turner opened his eyes again. Mitchell was still there. He had not moved. He was no doubt dead.

A yell came from downhill. It was Judge Topkah. 'Young man. Are you all right?'

Bill Turner stood up, dragged a shirtsleeve across his eyes and yelled back. 'Yes, I'm all right. Mitchell is dead.'

The judge climbed the hill and knelt beside the body. He lifted the man's wrist and felt for a pulse. 'He's dead, all right. It was him or us. I'll attest to that.'

'Will you,' Turner asked in a shaky voice, 'will you search him?'

'You think he's carrying money he took from two murdered men, is that it?'

'Yes.'

'What if he isn't?'

Another chill went through Turner.

Could he have been wrong about Mitchell? All evidence pointed to Mitchell. Turner had had no doubt that he was guilty of a double murder. Until now. Now that he had killed the man, a cold doubt swept through him. Nothing is certain. Despite all the evidence, he could have been mistaken.

With a trembling voice, Turner pleaded, 'Please. Please search him.'

The dead man's eyes were open when the judge turned the body over. 'I don't like doing this,' Judge Topkah said, 'but I suppose someone has to do it.'

Hands went over the pockets, then patted the chest and waist. 'Here's something,' the judge said. He unbuttoned the dead man's shirt and uncovered a leather money belt. He unbuckled the belt and pulled it free of the body.

The judge looked up from his squatting position at Turner. 'I still don't like doing this, but as a jurist I must do many things I don't like.' He opened the belt and took out a sheaf of bills. Slowly, carefully, Judge Topkah counted the money.

'Twenty-two thousand and one hundred dollars,' he said.

Turner was breathing in shallow breaths.

'Is it—is twenty thousand dollars of it new money?'

The judge thumbed through the sheaf of bills. 'Most of it appears to be brand new.'

A loud sigh came from Turner. 'I was right. George Kemp told me my brother and Mike Mahoney were paid with money fresh from the mint. The bills are bound to have consecutive serial numbers. Bank officials can surely identify the bills.'

Still squatting, the judge counted the money again. 'You're right. The first twenty thousand dollars I counted is brand new money in numerical order. The next two thousand is in a different order.'

'Are you satisfied, your honor, that Mitchell murdered my brother and Mike Mahoney?'

Judge Topkah stood up. 'Tell me, young man, what made you suspicious of Mitchell in the first place?'

Turner regained control of his voice. 'It was the way they were killed. Both shot in the back. Mitchell said they were bushwhacked from the willows that grow along the nearby creek. He even had two empty shell casings to prove it. Your honor, you can pick up empty shell casings a lot of places. And a bushwhacker couldn't have hit them both dead centre in the back.'

'Hmmmm,' the judge said, rubbing his jaw.

'What happened is this, your honor. Mitchell was in the bank with George Kemp. He knew all about the transaction, and he knew my brother and his partner had twenty thousand dollars in their pockets. They took cash because they wanted to start buying horses and equipment right away. I found some penciled notes on the wall of their tent which indicated that.

'Mitchell followed them, out of sight, to their camp. When they saw him coming, they believed they had nothing to fear because they believed him an honest representative of the law. They would have been ready to defend themselves if anyone else had approached them then.

'That made it easy for Mitchell to ride up, dismount, then draw his pistol and order them to get their hands up and turn around. He shot them in the back, but he had to be quick on the trigger.

'At the sound of the first shot, the man not hit would immediately spin around. It would be a normal reaction. The fact that both were shot squarely in the back meant it took someone very fast with a gun.

'Mitchell was very fast with a gun. I was in the Spotted Pup Saloon only a few days ago when he fired three shots and killed three men almost as quickly as you can blink your eyes three times.'

'Hmmm,' said Judge Topkah. 'Yes, he had a reputation for that. That is why he was appointed deputy sheriff. He was good at putting the fear of the law into hoodlums. But he was too quick to shoot, in my estimation.'

'I'm sorry, your honor, that I got you into such a dangerous situation. I knew there was a chance he would try to shoot me, but I didn't think he would shoot at you too.'

'You're not entirely forgiven, young man, but I can think of no crime to charge you with.'

'Are you satisfied that Mitchell was guilty?'

'Hmmm, yes. I may have to insist on a coroner's inquest. Get the coroner here from the county seat. But this appears to be a closed case. Let's get back to town.'

They found the part-time deputy, and Judge Topkah ordered him to get a wagon and go after Mitchell's body. Bill Turner had his left arm back in the sling and was rubbing his left shoulder, wincing at the pain.

'And you, young man, you'd better get on that stage this morning and go have that shoulder looked at.'

Bill Turner managed a smile. 'Yes, sir.'

'You'd better stay in Colorado Springs a day or two, however, in case the coroner or the state authorities ask questions about what happened here. I think I can tell them everything they want to know, but they may want to question you too.'

'I'll stick around,' Bill Turner said.

'Good luck, young man.'

'Judge,' Turner said, his face serious, 'I want to thank you. Proper law will come to Cripple Creek soon and it will be because of men like yourself, men who are not afraid to shuck their judge's robes, roll up their sleeves and get in the middle of things.'

Judge Topkah chuckled. 'Yes, I can truly say that now that I have dodged bullets in the name of justice. Not many jurists can say that. But if you ever come back to Cripple Creek, young man, I'm going to pretend I don't know you.'

The judge was still chuckling when

Turner left.

Four passengers were ready when the concord pulled by a sixup stopped in front of the Bluebird Hotel. There were a miner in overalls, Joel Lancaster, Mrs. Mahoney and Bill Turner. And there was Rose Vandel.

'I heard you all were leaving,' Rose Vandel said. 'I came to wish you well.'

'I looked on the street for you,' said Mrs. Mahoney. 'I want to thank you for your kindness.' She kissed Rose Vandel on the cheek. 'I'll never forget you.'

The driver sat on his high seat and held the lines while his helper loaded their luggage in the boot at the back of the coach. When they were all aboard, he said, 'Gee up,' and the coach creaked and clattered up Bennett Avenue. The horses were traveling at a trot until they started up the long hill leading to Florissant. Then the driver allowed them to slow to a walk.

Bill Turner looked down from the hill at the town of Cripple Creek. 'I'm coming back here,' he said. 'I like this country and these people, and this town needs a doctor.'

'Is that what you are going to do with the proceeds from your share of the mine, Bill? Mr. Turner?' It was Mrs. Mahoney asking.

'Go to medical school?'

'Yes. I'm going to see that my folks have everything that money can buy to make them comfortable and use what's left to pay tuition and room and board. I'm finally going to medical school.'

The horses were blowing hard by the time they topped the hill. The driver stopped them for a moment and let them blow. Then he hollered gee up and cracked a long whip over their backs. Their team struck a fast trot, trace chains rattling. 'Git in thar, Prince. Duke. Git into them collars.'

'I'm coming back too,' Mrs. Mahoney said. 'This is beautiful country, and I just can't leave the graves unattended.'

'Perhaps we'll meet again, Mrs. Mahoney,' Bill Turner said.

'Oh yes, I hope we do. After a time, perhaps quite a long time, I hope you will come visit me in Kansas City.'

'I've been thinking about that,' said Bill Turner. 'You can count on it.'

Photoset, printed and bound in Great Britain by REDWOOD BURN LIMITED, Trowbridge, Wiltshire